"Why are you going to all this trouble?" Kate asked.
The smoldering look in T. R.'s eyes gave her the answer before his words did. "I think you know." he said softly. "I want you."

She let out a big shuddering breath, suddenly afraid, not of him but of herself. "You're honest, I'll admit that. But it's just that I don't want you."

"Sure you do."

One long, graceful finger brushed her cheek, and slowly, tantalizingly, traced her suddenly heated skin—over her cheekbone, around her jaw, along her chin. Everywhere he touched he left an exquisite tingling sensation in his wake. "You're just having a little war with yourself," he murmured.

"My war is with you," she answered, suddenly finding it difficult to breathe. "And believe me, you won't be the winner."

He raised his hand to her mouth and ran the pad of his thumb lightly across her lower lip. Then he brought his thumb to his own mouth and licked it slowly, his tongue taking time to savor the taste of her. He pinned her with his intense blue eyes and said, "Won't I?"

WHAT ARE *LOVESWEPT* ROMANCES?

They are stories of true romance and touching emotion. We believe those two very important ingredients are constants in our highly sensual and very believable stories in the *LOVESWEPT* line. Our goal is to give you, the reader, stories of consistently high quality that may sometimes make you laugh, sometimes make you cry, but are always fresh and creative and contain many delightful surprises within their pages.

Most romance fans read an enormous number of books. Those they truly love, they keep. Others may be traded with friends and soon forgotten. We hope that each *LOVESWEPT* romance will be a treasure—a "keeper." We will always try to publish

LOVE STORIES YOU'LL NEVER FORGET
BY AUTHORS YOU'LL ALWAYS REMEMBER

The Editors

Diane Pershing

Satisfaction

BANTAM BOOKS

NEW YORK • TORONTO • LONDON • SYDNEY • AUCKLAND

SATISFACTION

A Bantam Book / May 1993

To Diane Wehner,
Ruth Brodie, and
Chuck Bernstein—
my experts,
my friends

One

"Excuse me, would you mind bringing me a towel?"

The woman's voice came from somewhere behind him, thought T. R., as he continued to maneuver the long umbrella pole deeper into the sand. It was a pleasant voice, low and throaty, and merged easily with the gentle lapping of waves at the shoreline, the twittering of birds carried from far away by the warm Hawaiian breeze, and somewhere on the beach, the soft thud of a bass from a radio.

"How's that?" T. R. asked the elderly man he'd seen struggling to set up the umbrella. "Enough shade?"

"Yes, thank you," the man said gratefully. "You've been most helpful."

"Excuse me." It was the woman behind him again. "I'm sorry to be so impatient, but I seem to have something in my eye."

Her tone was more insistent now. T. R. turned to see who she was talking to.

Lying on one of the hotel's chaises was a lady in a slinky gold bikini, huge sunglasses, and a straw hat. Nice body, more than nice actually, and she was looking in his direction, though it was hard to tell if, behind the shades, she was looking at him for sure.

He pointed to his chest. "Are you talking to me?"

She nodded. "I need a towel. Isn't that part of your job?"

Actually, no, it wasn't part of his job, not in the least. He'd obviously been put into the beachboy-help category. Only a few years ago, he might have felt insulted that this obviously well-to-do lady had mistaken him for the minimum-wage hired help.

Now, excusing her, he acknowledged that he probably appeared as exotic as a lot of the natives. His skin was even darker than usual from this week in the sun, and with his long black hair worn in a ponytail, he supposed if you had something in your eye and you weren't seeing too well, you could—even though he was well into his thirties—mistake him for one of the teenagers who brought towels, chairs, umbrellas, and drinks to the hotel's customers.

He trotted over to a large woven basket in the shade of a palm tree and picked up a couple of thick towels. Then he trotted back to the lady in the bikini, puffing out his chest so any extra thickness around his waistline and gut would be moved upward, and offered her the towels.

"Thank you," she said, taking one and reaching up under the sunglasses to wipe at her eye.

"My pleasure." Bowing slightly, T. R. turned to leave. He'd been on his way off the beach when the old man had asked for his help, and he really needed to go. It was all well and good to lounge around on a summer's day and admire the occasional spectacular body, but he had other business today.

"Don't I have to sign for the towel?" she asked. "Give you my room number, or something?"

He turned back as the woman removed her sunglasses and looked up at him.

"Holy sh—" He wasn't sure if he'd spoken out loud, but he had the presence of mind to stop himself before he could finish the phrase.

Kate O'Brien.

It was Kate O'Brien he'd been talking to, who was sitting right here in front of him on a beach in Hawaii.

Like a movie, quick flashbacks from his youth crossed through his mind's eye, scenes from his one semester in a southern California high school. Culver High.

Cheerleaders with short skirts. Katie O'Brien in the center.

Push 'em back, push 'em back, waaay back.

Katie did or Katie didn't, the kids used to say.

Kate O'Brien, luscious Kate—thick blond hair, translucent blue-gray eyes, great jugs. He winced—what a horrible word for this most delectable part of a woman's anatomy. But there had been a lot of words like that then, spoken by the pimply-faced boys hanging around the locker room, bragging and lying about who got into whose pants. He'd been only one of the many hot and horny boys who admired her, who loved to watch her breasts bounce in her cheerleader sweater, who dreamed of how it would be to lie between her legs. Lord, he'd wanted her.

From afar, of course. Everything was from afar in those days. He doubted Kate would even remember him at all.

"*Do* I have to sign something?" she asked again. "It's my first day here, and I'm not sure about protocol."

Kate wondered why the beachboy wasn't answering her questions. She craned her neck to look up at him, but even with the dark glasses back in place, she was forced to squint. The bright

Hawaiian sun, especially strong in August, made viewing difficult. She could just discern the boy's outline—a nice muscular outline. An inch or two under six feet. And, of course, the symbol of freedom or rebellion, or whatever it was—long black hair tied back with a shoelace.

The boy—or was he a man? She was beginning to think she might have misjudged his age—squatted suddenly next to her chair. At eye level, she could see him now without having to squint.

"I don't know the protocol either," he said. "But I imagine you don't have to account for all the towels you use here. You're supposed to hang loose when you're on vacation."

He had the most interesting eyes, Kate thought. They were a deeper blue than hers, a true cornflower blue, set in startlingly white irises. Against the dark honey skin tones of his face, his eyes were mesmerizing. He also had high, almost oriental cheekbones and a high-bridged nose that had been broken a few times but managed to look sexy instead of disfigured.

"I think you've mistaken me for one of the beachboys who work here," he said with an easy, open grin. "I'm afraid I'm not."

Kate's hand flew to her mouth with embarrassment. "I'm so sorry. I thought you were—Well, you're dressed like they are, I mean your bathing suit is—"

She couldn't finish her sentence because she wasn't about to say she'd noticed that his black briefs were just that, brief, barely adequate enough to conceal anything. And she'd looked.

"—With your hair and all," she went on, feeling lame and stupid. "I'm so sorry."

He laughed, a nice rich laugh. "You're forgiven. In fact, you've made my day. But I am not a native Hawaiian. Actually, my heritage is Cherokee, Irish, and Mexican—with a Greek grandfather thrown in, it's rumored. And," he added, "I am no longer a boy."

He spoke with a slow, lazy rhythm. And was there a slight accent? Hispanic, she thought, a softness on the consonants. The sound was sensual, caressing, and came out of a beautifully shaped mouth, with deliciously full lips.

She was attracted to him, she realized, and the thought made her vaguely uncomfortable. But why? she asked herself. There was nothing wrong with a strong physical attraction to a stranger . . . was there?

She wished she weren't wearing this damned bikini. She'd been talked into it by one of her clients, Sybil Conn. Hearing that Kate and her daughter, Dee, were off to this particular resort, Sybil had brought in a bunch of very expensive, slightly used clothing from her own closet. While she'd been uncertain about whether or not to accept Sybil's largess, Kate had finally agreed that to attract the right kind of man, she needed the right kind of clothing.

And here she was, on day one of her treasured trip, talking to a man. And attracting him, too, it appeared. Unfortunately, her gut was telling her that he was not the right kind at all. He looked like an outlaw, and he was too . . . sensual.

She fought down the urge to fold her arms over her chest, or pull up her suit bottom so that more of her stomach was covered. There were faint stretch marks there, and although she wasn't exactly ashamed of them, she sure did wish there were an inch or two more material all around.

She watched, mute, as the stranger's gaze swept over her, from her painted toenails up to her hat, stopping to rest briefly on various highlights along the way. She was being given the once-over. But rather than bristle and make a sarcastic remark to him, as as she would to another man, she found herself waiting for him to finish his journey along her flesh so she could read what was in his eyes.

When he met her gaze, there was a breath-stopping moment as neither of them blinked. A surge of sizzling electricity went through Kate, and she wondered if he could feel it, too, then decided that of course he could; that kind of reaction was never one-way.

"Nice suit," he said finally.

"If you go in for the less-is-more type of thing, I guess it is," she replied, wondering if her voice sounded as breathless to him as it did to her.

He smiled, a lazy, knowing grin, and continued to look at her with frank approval, man to woman. There was no sense of threat from him, no feeling of being thought of as an object.

She liked his body a whole lot too. And as he'd said, he was definitely not a boy.

Rising out of his crouch, the man sat himself down on the empty lounge next to her and faced her, his elbows resting easily on his knees. "Mind if I visit for a minute?"

"Well," she said, bringing her chair up to a sitting position so she would feel a little less exposed, "I'm expecting someone else."

"Husband? Boyfriend?"

"You get right to it, don't you?"

He looked taken aback for a moment, then he laughed, his strong white teeth gleaming in the afternoon sunlight. "I'm being obvious, huh?"

She joined in his laughter. "Your eyes are. I feel a little like the main course at a feast," she said. "And I don't even know your name."

"Sorry, but you're real easy to look at. Besides, if you don't want male appreciation, you shouldn't dress like that."

"Give the man first prize," she said, reaching for her beach bag. "I couldn't agree more. I'll cover up."

"No, please."

The mock panic on his face made her laugh and sit back again. "Okay. I won't."

"I'm T. R." he said.

"Pardon?"

"That's my name. T period R period."

"I'll bet that's not what's on your birth certificate."

"You'd win the bet," he said easily. "And you're Kate, Kate O'Brien. At least it used to be."

His comment took her completely by surprise. "How do you know who I am?"

"Culver High, nineteen years ago."

"Culver High. Yes, I went there." She squinted at him again, trying to remember his face. He didn't look even vaguely familiar. "Were you T. R. then too?"

"No. Tomás. Tomás Ryan Beltran."

She shook her head. "I'm sorry, I don't remember you."

So, she didn't recognize him, T. R. thought, as a swift wave of disappointment swept over him. Not from all those years ago, or from more recent times, either. He hoped his feeling of being let down didn't show on his face. "No reason you should, really. I was a senior when you were a sophomore. And I was only there a few months."

Even so, he'd always had a fantasy that he'd been more important to her than he'd realized at the time, and that maybe she, too, remembered him and wished they'd gotten to know each other better.

Zap. End of that fantasy.

"It was quite a jolt seeing you here today," he said.

"How come you remember me?"

"Are you kidding? You were one of the most popular girls in the school. Great grades, great-looking. You were going with some guy, Alan something. A trombone player."

"Yes, Alan something. That about covers it." She

could hear the dismissal in her voice, but there was no way she was going to let that jerk Alan intrude on her vacation, not after all these years.

"Is it still Kate O'Brien?" T. R. asked.

"Is *what* still Kate O'Brien?"

"Your name."

"Oh. Yes, it is."

He was not too subtly fishing around for her marital status, which would lead to sharing their stories, which would lead to . . . what did she want it to lead to?

She pulled her sunglasses down to the bridge of her nose and peered over the top of them. "Are you trying to pick me up, by any chance?" she asked.

He grinned. "You get right to it, too, don't you?"

"I've been known to say what's on my mind," she said lightly. "Are you?"

"How can you pick up someone you've known for nineteen years?"

"I could quibble with that statement, but you have a point." She felt one corner of her mouth turn up as she realized she was really enjoying this conversation. Something about T. R. made him easy to talk to. "Where did you go after Culver?" she asked.

"Let me see, I think it was Guam."

"Guam?"

"Yeah, we traveled a lot. I was a military brat."

"That's a hard life, isn't it?"

He shrugged. "You learn to be self-sufficient, I'll say that."

And lonely, he added silently, and hard, and certain that there's no such thing as permanence in the world. But he didn't say any of that out loud. It didn't go with the warm, sunny day and the gorgeous woman just inches away from him. He shook his head. Hot damn, he said to himself, just think of it—sitting on a beach in Hawaii, talking to Kate O'Brien!

He wondered what her situation was, both marital and economic. She had money, of course—she was the type who married well or had a thriving career. He'd seen a bikini just like hers on the beach in Cannes last year. And no one could afford to stay at this posh resort on the Big Island unless they were rolling in the bucks. Even a small room was several hundred dollars a day.

"How do you like the hotel?" he asked.

"It's lovely. I have a great room overlooking the ocean." Pushing her sunglasses back up so they covered her eyes, Kate turned her face up to the sun. "Are you staying here too?" she asked.

"Uh, no. Nearby."

"I see."

"I didn't sneak onto the property or anything like that," he said.

She angled her head toward him, looking surprised. "I didn't think you had."

Of course she hadn't. He had jumped to defend himself in a way he hadn't—hadn't *had* to—for years. Seeing Kate O'Brien was taking him back to the days when he yearned to feel a part of something but didn't know how—the old trespasser reaction again.

"I'm staying at a friend's place, one of the condos next door," he offered. "It's part of the whole resort."

"Oh."

He waited for her to ask what he did for a living, but she didn't. It was one of the first questions women usually posed, so they could assess the amount of power and/or money a man had. Then he berated himself for being cynical. Not all women were like that—so maybe Kate O'Brien wasn't.

He lay back on his lounge and closed his eyes against the midday sun. "So, how do you like Hawaii so far?"

"I love it," Kate said. "I think we should make it a state."

He smiled. He didn't remember her having such a sense of humor. But then, in the old days, he'd never really talked to her, had he? "It's a whole other world than L.A., isn't it? Do you still live there?"

"Yes. We got here last night," she murmured, "and the minute I got off the plane, my shoulders unclenched. It's so relaxing, even after a mere twelve hours. By the end of the week, I should be ready to float away."

We got here, she'd said. "Yeah, it's like that, isn't it? And this island is better than most—fewer tourists, fewer activities. Have you been to any others? Maui? Oahu?"

"Nope, this is our first time."

Our first time. Who was the other person who would soon be sitting on this chair?

As if to answer his question, a tall, skinny girl with very white skin and very red hair that stuck up in spikes came running up. She wore a turquoise gauze cover-up over a black one-piece bathing suit, and carried a large boom box and a set of earphones.

"Mom, there you are," the girl said, setting her stuff down next to Kate's chair. "I've been looking all over for you. Isn't this place cool? It's so big. And did you see the dolphins? I—" She stopped talking as she finally noticed T. R. Like a gangly young bird, she stood still, her head cocked to one side. "Do I know you?"

Kate rose up to a sitting position. "Dee, meet T. R. T. R., this is my daughter, Dee."

"T. R.? Cool name." Dee sat on the edge of her mother's lounge chair and studied him. She had her mother's eyes, and they dominated her face. "I've always wanted a cool name. You look kind of familiar."

"Do I?" he said, noncommittally.

"Yeah. How do you know Mom?"

"Dee," Kate said mildly, "cut out the third degree."

T. R. smiled. "It's okay. Your mom and I went to high school together."

"No kidding?"

He made himself sit up, then got up off the chaise. "This is your seat, I think. Unless your father is coming too."

"My father? Did you know him?"

Her question threw him. "I don't think so."

"No, he didn't," Kate said firmly.

T. R. couldn't help noticing that the father was referred to in the past tense. Interesting.

Dee rose and pulled off her cover-up. "I'm going into the ocean," she announced.

"Be careful, please."

"Mom, I've been swimming since I was a baby."

"Silly me, I forgot." Kate smiled. "It just slipped out. Sorry."

Dee ran off on impossibly long legs, like a young deer. T. R. noted that Kate's wisecracking facade completely disappeared when she looked at her daughter. In its place was unguarded, vulnerable mother love. Nice.

He sat down again. "She's quite a kid."

"Thanks," she said quietly. "I got lucky."

"What is she—fourteen? Fifteen?"

"She just turned sixteen," Kate answered.

"You're kidding."

"She's a little late developing. I'm glad about that even if she isn't. Poor baby, she's so impatient."

"Sixteen? That means you had her—"

"Very young. Yes."

Hoping to give T. R. a hint that she was not really in the mood to talk about her extremely early introduction to motherhood—she barely knew him, after all—Kate leaned back and closed her eyes again.

"So, it's just the two of you here in Hawaii, then?"

"Yes, Dee and I are here alone."

"I'm here alone too."

"What an amazing coincidence," she said dryly.

"Anyone back home? A man, I mean."

She wished they could stay at the bantering stage for a little longer; this was definitely turning into a pickup, whatever T. R. wanted to call it. Still, she always tried to give a direct answer to a direct question. "No, there is no man in my life, here or there."

"The news pleases me greatly."

"Glad to be of service."

He grinned, that lazy, confident grin she was already used to, though they'd only been talking for a few minutes. "How about meeting me for a drink later," he said, "and telling me the story of your life?"

She laughed. He really was quite a charmer. "That would take more than one drink."

"Okay, several then. I don't have to be anywhere for a while. As a matter of fact, I could show you the island—you and your daughter, I mean. There's a great cattle ranch and a volcano, and some waterfalls that'll blow you away, they're so beautiful."

"Thanks, but no thanks."

He seemed taken aback by her answer. "How come?"

She wondered herself why she'd turned him down so quickly. Was it because he was moving too fast for her? Or because that vague sense of discomfort about being attracted to him was less vague now? Some warning was nibbling at the edge of her consciousness, something she couldn't quite put her finger on. . . .

"I want to spend a lot of time with Dee," Kate said finally, which was true, even if it wasn't the main reason.

"You'll be lucky if you see her after today. The kids here tend to find each other and hang out on the beach all day and evening, listening to music. You'll be in the way, trust me."

"You're probably right," she admitted. "It's just that—"

"I know," he said, interrupting her. "I'm going too fast, aren't I? Forget what I said about showing you the island, okay? I was planning ahead, and that's not the Hawaiian way. Meet me for one drink, this evening. After that, we'll play it by ear."

It was amazing how he'd read her mood and slowed his pace. One drink, Kate said to herself. How could that hurt? She'd meet him for one drink this evening and then discourage any further familiarity. Although she couldn't say exactly why, a gut feeling told her to stay away from this man— far, far away.

Still, one drink would be okay. She was on vacation. Didn't she deserve a *little* fun?

"I'm still not sure," she said honestly.

"Then I guess I'll stay here till you are," T. R. announced, leaning back on the chaise. "I have all the time in the world."

Confident devil, she thought, unable to suppress the flush of pleasure she felt at his persistence, even as she sought to distance herself from him. Push-pull. Flip-flop. Nothing like consistency, O'Brien.

"Are you in Hawaii on vacation or work?" she asked.

"Yes."

"Care to elaborate?"

"Nope."

"My, my. A mystery man."

She was right, of course, T. R. admitted. He *was* being mysterious. He was glad to talk about the old days but was reluctant to part with any current information about himself because . . .

Because he wanted Kate O'Brien.

And he wanted her to want to be with him, just him, without any trappings, without her knowing about his fame, his wealth, anything.

He wanted to turn back the clock to nineteen

years ago, when he was still a solitary, unhappy nobody, the mongrel son of an alcoholic military man, and he wanted Kate O'Brien to want him anyway.

Talk about not giving up on a fantasy.

"Mystery is my middle name," he said. "But, meet me for a drink and I'll tell all . . . well, almost all," he added.

Kate caught the shuttered look on T. R.'s face. He had secrets too. Lord, the world was filled with people and their secrets. "You're trying to bribe me now," she said, smiling. "Bad form."

"I'm not a criminal, I'm not married, I'm not gay, and I'm good with children and animals," he said in his slow, caressing way. "What else do you need to know?"

"Not much, I admit."

"Then it's settled."

He rose from the chair and stood over her, dangerously, disturbingly close, and immediately her body shifted subtly into tingling awareness of him, of his nearly nude golden-brown form, with its sturdy yet sleek musculature.

"How's five o'clock in the Kulani Lounge?" he said.

She tried not to focus on any part of him but his face, but he radiated maleness as the sun radiated heat, and she was drawn to him against her will. *Danger ahead,* she told herself, but her mouth formed the words, "Five o'clock is fine. I'll be there."

He put his hand on her shoulder and squeezed gently. "Good," he said, his thumb rubbing lightly over a small patch of skin.

The touch of flesh on flesh seared her with its intensity. She shivered involuntarily and looked at his hand on her shoulder, dark honey against white. He had long, graceful fingers, not thick like the rest of him, but sensitive, artistic.

Artistic?

A new warning bell went off in her head. She looked up at him again, suddenly not sure she should have agreed to meet him.

Some trepidation must have shown on her face because he dropped his hand and turned up the corners of his mouth reassuringly. "I know we moved right along, but you and I go way back, Kate. School loyalty should count for something."

"Rah, rah, rah," she said absently, not really hearing the words as she studied him.

She could see it now, the reason for her discomfort, and wondered why she'd failed to notice it before. Behind the easy charm lurked something wild and wicked, something free of societal restraint, a disdain for order. Untamed and untamable.

And those hands—they could belong to a surgeon. Or a sculptor. Or a . . .

"By any chance, are you a musician?" she asked.

The grin left his face, and he stared at her for a moment, the shuttered look back in his half-lidded eyes. "Why do you want to know?"

"Why don't you want to tell me?"

He shrugged. "Something to do with wanting to be liked for what I am, not what I do."

She drew in a breath. Oh my, did she understand what he meant, only too well. Still, she needed to know. "Nice thought," she said. "Honest too. But I'd still like an answer."

"Some women have this thing about musicians," he went on. "They crawl all over them. But if you're a plumber or you set up pins in a bowling alley, they don't crawl so fast. I don't like this status thing, you know?"

"I have no plans to crawl over you either way," Kate said more pointedly. "So, which is it? Plumber or music man?"

What was he doing? T. R. asked himself. The mysterious bit went only so far; now she was getting annoyed, and he didn't really blame her.

It had to come out sooner or later, he told himself, so cut the crap.

Raising his hands in a gesture of surrender, he said, "Okay, you win. I *am* a musician."

"Of course you are." Kate shook her head slowly and, as though she were admonishing herself, said quietly, "I should have known."

"What do you mean by that?"

She expelled an impatient breath. "I'm sorry, you're wasting your time."

Two

"Wasting my time?" T. R. said.

She'd done it again, she told herself. Terrific. Way to go, Kate.

Getting up quickly from her chaise, she threw on a lacy cover-up. "You've got the wrong woman," she said abruptly. "I don't go out with musicians."

"Why? You too good for them?"

She glanced at him, noting the cynical mistrust on his face. It was the first time he'd shown her anything other than a sort of casual cockiness. She must have struck a nerve, she told herself. But that wasn't her problem.

Shaking her head, she threw her sunscreen, keys, and tissues into her large straw purse, then looked around for anything else she might have forgotten. "No, I don't mean that at all. It's just that I've had a couple of bad experiences with musicians, okay? And I make it a policy to learn from my experiences."

T. R. crossed his arms and studied her, frowning. Why had she shut down so suddenly, he wondered, so completely? It was as if a light had gone off.

"And that's it? Some lousy dates and you swear off a whole segment of the population for life?"

"That's about it, in a nutshell."

"My God, what did those guys do to you?"

She stopped her packing-up activity for a moment, then said thoughtfully, "I guess it wasn't what they did, but what they didn't do." She looked at him and shrugged. "And I don't want to go into it, not right now, if you don't mind. I'm not rejecting you, really."

"Uh-huh."

"I mean, don't take it personally."

"Bull!" he exploded. "Don't take it personally, huh? Well, listen, Kate—"

He was about to tell her that she was mistaking him for the stereotype of the typical musician—one of those always broke but always high, fancy-free-type dudes who live for their music and nothing else, like the Jeff Bridges character in *The Fabulous Baker Boys*. Sure, that was it. She'd probably had a roll in the hay with a guy in a band who didn't call her back the next day.

He wanted to tell her that he used to be one of those guys. But then he'd hit it big and had a very successful career, thank you very much. She couldn't dismiss him that easily.

He wanted to tell her that he could have women—beautiful, desirable women—anytime he wanted, and she could take her blanket condemnation and—

But he stopped himself from saying any of that because he knew he was overreacting, and when he got like this, he tended to lash out and say hurtful things, things he didn't even believe. Besides, Kate looked as if she had a pretty good temper on her, too, and they might end up in a screaming match . . . instead of on a soft mattress, which was what he had decided they were going to do, as soon as possible.

The thing was, he really wanted her—even more

now that there was a real challenge to getting her. Maybe he was giving in to a need, maybe even a pathetic need, to reinvent his past. So what? Whatever his reasons, he was going to have her, the blond, blue-eyed golden girl of his youth.

And he wanted her on his terms. Yeah. He wanted Kate O'Brien to think he was a loser . . . and come to him anyway.

He took a deep, relaxing breath and uncrossed his arms from their defensive stance. Patience, he told himself. Anything worthwhile is worth waiting for.

Resting a foot on her chaise, he leaned an elbow on his knee and lifted the corners of his mouth. "Truce, okay?"

T. R. was doing his charming bit again, Kate thought. And, boy, was he good at it! But it would have no effect, as he would find out. "Sure, truce. But I won't be meeting you for a drink. I really am sorry, but I meant what I said."

"Not even as friends?"

"Come on, T. R. You don't look at me like you mean friendship."

"You're right, I'll give you that. But"—he gazed at her through half-lidded eyes as he continued softly—"I could say the same about you, Kate. I think our attraction is mutual. And we could have a hell of a lot of fun."

His message was clear; those astonishing blue eyes under heavy lids promised sensual, erotic pleasures probably not in her experience. She sighed. It was too bad, but there was no way— no way at all. "Sorry," she said, "I've developed an allergy to fun."

She could see a small muscle in his jaw tighten, but it was gone in an instant. Removing his foot from her lounge chair, he lifted his hands in a gesture of surrender. "Well, I guess I can't fight city hall. Stay here on the beach, spend some time with your daughter. You don't have to pack up to get away from me. I was leaving anyway. See you around."

And, with a quick wave and a cocky grin, he was gone, striding off on strong, well-shaped legs. Exceptionally nice buns, Kate noted as she experienced a sharp sense of loss at his departure. She had pictured herself as the one to walk off, and it didn't feel right to have *him* leave *her,* especially with such a casual "See you around." It was as if he didn't really care that she'd turned him down.

Stop it, she told herself, that was pure vanity. She'd told him to get lost and he had. Then why wasn't she feeling relief that he was gone and had gone quietly? It was unsettling. T. R. was unsettling.

Another musician, she thought with disgust, as she removed her cover-up and lay back down on the chaise. She'd been lightning-bolt attracted to another musician, a word synonymous with love 'em and leave 'em. Twice, in her case—not just Dee's biological father, Alan, but also the man Kate had married a few years later, the man she'd thought would supply Dee with a loving stepfather, and herself with some sense of belonging somewhere.

Both of these men—well, boys, really—had been seduced by the wandering life they chose to lead, the one-night stands in a band, and the one-night stands in beds other than Kate's.

She was done with that kind of man forever, she told herself firmly. She was determined, once and for all, to meet a grown-up, a guy with a steady job, maybe a little in his savings account. He didn't have to be wealthy, but he did have to be reliable. She no longer required charisma or sex appeal, but she did require constancy. She wanted a man who was present and accounted for, especially when she needed him.

So what if conversation between them didn't sparkle with underlying sexual tension and playfulness? So what if there weren't any fireworks in bed? So what if he didn't have long, graceful fingers that played soft melodies on her flesh?

She'd had that, and it had ended in heartbreak, both times.

"Where did T. R. go, Mom?"

Kate's reverie was interrupted by Dee, who was standing over her and dripping droplets of the Pacific on her bare skin. "Dee, you're wet!"

"Of course I am. I've been in the ocean."

Kate looked up at her daughter. "I've been noticing a little sarcasm creeping into your delivery lately. You're too young."

"Am I?" Dee grinned as she spread her towel over the cushion now vacated by T. R. "According to Grandma, you were born with a smart mouth. I have to catch up."

"Ignore your grandmother. She tends to be Pollyanna. Anything other than sweetness and angelic smiles means you're hostile."

As her daughter lay down, Kate looked over at her, aware that she was smiling the fond smile that mothers get. Dee really was a great kid. Enthusiastic and loving. The two of them were very close, able to talk easily, without the strain that so many mothers and daughters experienced.

And thank God Dee was starting to display two budding breasts. They'd actually gone bra-shopping last week. Thirty-two Triple-A. Dee had reached her height of five feet eight two years ago; it looked like the rest of her would start to catch up now.

"So, where is he?" Dee asked.

"Who?"

"You know who. T. R."

"I have no idea." Kate fished in her straw purse for a magazine and leafed through the pages. In the clothing ads, most of the models were around Dee's age. Not a wrinkle or a stretch mark in sight. It was depressing.

"Are you going to see him again?"

"I don't know," she said, keeping her tone neutral. "He's staying in a condo next door."

"He was cool. Buff body, for an old guy."

"Positively ancient. All of thirty-five, probably."

"Yeah. Well, I liked him."

"How could you?" Kate said. "You exchanged two words with him."

Dee shrugged. "Words aren't the big thing. It's all about vibes."

"He's too old for you."

"Mom! Not for me, for you."

"Me? Bite your tongue." Kate tried to concentrate on the article she was reading, but Dee's words were keeping T. R.'s face in front of her instead.

"He has great eyes." Dee sighed meaningfully. "Soulful."

"Sorry, honey, he's not my type."

"What is your type? You hardly ever go out."

"What is this? The third degree?"

"Well, I wonder, that's all. I mean, I know you have a lot of responsibilities. But you also have, well, you know, like, *needs*."

Kate glanced up from her magazine at her fresh-faced daughter. Dee was giving her a look that Kate could remember from infancy—tentative but obstinate. "Needs," she repeated with a small smile. "I think my needs, at least the ones you're referring to, are my business."

Two spots of color rose on Dee's cheeks. "Hey, I'm not asking you to, you know, give me details of your sex life. But you're too stressed at home. We're on vacation. You should, like, lighten up a little."

Kate bit her lip to keep from laughing aloud at her daughter's lecture. She supposed she would be getting more and more of them; at Dee's age, Kate had thought she knew everything too. "I'm trying, sweetheart, I promise. Right now, I'm concentrating on relaxing, getting some sun, and turning off my head. May I, please?"

"Sure. No prob."

Kate let her magazine drop and adjusted her chair so she could lie back again.

Dee reached down and brought her radio up next to her. "T. R.," she said musingly. "Wonder what that stands for?"

"Tomás something."

"He really does look familiar, Mom. Does he live in L.A.?"

"I have no idea. And I have no more information for you, so it won't do any good to ask more questions, okay?"

Dee let out a big dramatic sigh that said she really did have a lot to put up with, and placed her earphones on her head. The sound of drums and cymbals, a clanging guitar, and a singer who managed to whine at the same time he was shouting, poured forth from Dee's boom box.

Kate reached over and patted her on the shoulder. Dee opened her eyes and raised her eyebrows at her mother.

"Turn it down," Kate said, knowing Dee would have to read her lips because of the cacophony currently pouring into her eardrums.

Dee made a face but lowered the volume. "You'd better be grateful I listen to this stuff. If I didn't, we wouldn't be here," she pronounced with a triumphant smile. She lay back down, her unmarked young face once again absorbed in listening while her slender body moved in time to the music.

Kate smiled to herself. Her daughter was right, of course. Dee had won this trip for two to a luxurious Hawaiian resort on her favorite local L.A. radio station by correctly identifying ten different guitarists after listening to ten seconds of playing by each of them. Her daughter's ear was amazing, and so was her singing voice, Kate had to admit with a mixture of pride, exasperation, and a little fear. Dee had inherited her father's musicality; Kate sincerely hoped it would remain a hobby.

Once again, she lay back and closed her eyes,

sighing as a warm tropical breeze swept over her, bringing with it the dark, sweet smell of orchids. Hang loose, she told herself, that was the Hawaiian way. All the tension, the money worries, Dee's future, Mom's emphysema, her own loneliness and needs—let them all float away on the breeze.

Hang loose.

She felt herself drifting off to the sound of children playing at the shoreline, and someone on Dee's radio crooning about unrequited love.

"So, Margaret and I decided that twenty years together was enough. I get Tod every other weekend and half of all vacations. I have to say, Margaret's been great about the whole thing."

Kate nodded, hoping that George Bierman couldn't tell that she was listening to him with only half her brain.

They were sitting at a table in the Kulani Lounge, a large outdoor dining room filled with rattan tables and chairs and protected from Hawaii's frequent afternoon rains by a canvas covering. Kate found herself fascinated by the small birds that kept flying through the room, hopping occasionally onto a table for a bread crumb. No one bothered them or shooed them away; it would have required too much effort. As she nibbled on the sweetest, most delectable pineapple she'd ever tasted, Kate agreed that any extraneous movement was a waste of time.

George, the man sitting across from her, was in his early forties, with thinning brown hair and thick-lensed aviator glasses. Decent-looking and polite, he'd come up to her a half hour ago as she sat nursing a glass of juice. He'd told her he was here at the resort with his son, had seen her on the beach that morning, and wondered if he could join her. She'd said yes. George gave off the impression of rock-solid reliability; he was just the kind of man she was determined to have in her life.

If only all these pesky thoughts of T. R. would vanish from her head. After that nice nap she'd had in the sunshine, the only thing interfering with her present peace of mind was the memory of a black-haired outlaw with impossibly sultry blue eyes.

"How about you?" George asked. "Ever been married?"

"Once," Kate said. "A while ago. It didn't take."

"Divorce is rough. It takes a lot out of you." George studied the table for a moment, then looked up and smiled. "But, enough of that, right? I've been talking your ear off."

"It's all right."

He pointed to her empty glass. "How about if I stop talking and buy you another drink instead?"

He had a very nice face, Kate thought. Kind. Settled. Why in heaven's name didn't it appeal to her? "I'd like that very much," she said, smiling. Maybe if she acted as if she were attracted to him, she'd find she was.

"I'll mosey on over to the bar," George said, getting up a bit clumsily "and pick out something exotic, with umbrellas and things. Is that okay with you?"

He looked eager, a little like a cocker spaniel she'd once had who loved to be petted but didn't know when to stop begging. It was not an overly attractive quality in a man, Kate thought. But George was definitely a man; she couldn't help noticing how his eyes kept straying to her cleavage.

She was wearing a halter-topped sundress of coral cotton, another of Sybil's offerings. The problem was that Sybil's clothing was cut a little lower and a little tighter around the bustline than Kate was used to.

Fighting down the urge to splay her hand over

her chest, she said, "Umbrellas and things sound fine, George. Thanks."

She watched him as he walked off. Thin legs, slightly bowed, very hairy, very white. Glimpses of thickly muscled bronze thighs and calves came into her head like naughty postcards. T. R.'s thighs and calves, as a matter of fact. Stop it, she told herself. You're letting your hormones go into overdrive.

"Mom! There you are."

Kate looked around at the sound of Dee's voice. Her daughter was waving to her as she strode up, followed by—

Oh, no!

"Look who I found," Dee said enthusiastically. "I was heading toward the little room where they have Ping-Pong stuff, and T. R. was jamming away at the piano bar. He let me sing a little bit, and he played something he's working on."

Dee paused for a deep breath, then said reverently, "He's a *musician*, Mom."

"So I've been informed."

T. R. stood just behind her daughter, wearing a short-sleeved cotton shirt—black palm trees on a burnt-orange background—over the same black briefs he'd had on earlier. The shirt's color gave a warm brandy tinge to his skin, and, unbuttoned as it was, did nothing to hide the broad expanse of his pectorals or upper arms. From a purely objective point of view, Kate had to admit, the man was a hunk, no doubt about it.

However, her reaction to him was far from objective. There were funny, tingly sensations happening to her breasts and the muscles deep within her womb, at the sight of him. Dammit. She was trying to get to know George, and T. R. was distracting. Why did he have to show up now?

"He's played *gigs*," Dee said, her eyes shining, "and he's been on the road and all that stuff."

"How nice for him." In spite of her heated reaction, Kate managed at least to keep her voice cool.

T. R. gave Kate a shrewd smile. "That bit of information is more pleasing to you, Dee, than to your mother."

Dee collapsed on the chair next to Kate, her long legs sprawled out in front of her. "Oh, you know moms. They don't like to hear you getting all buzzed about music. You're supposed to take a typing class, or get a teaching credential. 'You'll never make anything of yourself without an education.' Blah blah blah."

"She's right about that, let me tell you," T. R. said, folding his arms across his chest. "Getting an education is the most important thing a kid can do."

Kate was surprised to hear her own belief echoed by T. R. Maybe it wouldn't be two against one, on this subject, at least.

Dee made a face. "Not you too," she groaned. "You mean, you went to college?"

"I never graduated from high school."

"See?" Dee turned to her mother in triumph. "Who needs it?"

"Why didn't you graduate?" Kate found herself asking, drawn by some undercurrent in T. R.'s tone. "Unless it's too personal, of course."

"It's okay. I had a chance to go on the road with a band. At the time, it seemed the most important thing in the world." He paused and smiled ruefully. "Now, it's one of the biggest regrets I have."

There was no self-pity in his voice, but Kate could sense pain in there, pain she understood very well. She wanted to know more about his pain, about what made him tick. She was intrigued by the man, drawn to him in spite of herself. "It's not too late to go back," she said, "if it really means that much to you."

He shrugged. "Yeah, I guess so," he said with a notable lack of enthusiasm.

The softening she'd felt toward him evaporated instantly. Sure, she thought darkly, tell someone like T. R. to go back to cracking the books and getting up early and meeting deadlines. Tell that to a guy who's probably used to crawling out of a bed—and probably not his own—at two in the afternoon. Sure.

The suddenly bitter direction of her thoughts took Kate by surprise; she'd thought she was over those old disappointments and past hurts. Shaking herself mentally, she admonished herself not to dwell on ancient history, just as good ol' George—as she was already thinking of him—came back with the drinks. They were enormous foamy pink concoctions, replete with not only umbrellas, but pineapple slices, cherries, and a thick yellow banana sticking out of the center in such a way that Kate forced herself to look down at the table, afraid she was about to erupt in a sudden attack of nervous giggles.

Yes, her hormones were certainly on overdrive; she needed them to go back into park.

When she'd recovered her composure, Kate raised her eyes again to find T. R. studying her, a knowing smile curving his sensuous mouth. She pointedly turned her attention to George, whose eyes were darting back and forth between the two newcomers.

"George Bierman," Kate said, "this is my daughter, Dee, and T. R.—what did you say your last name was?"

"Just T. R.," he replied easily, pulling up another chair and settling himself a few inches from her.

George set down the drinks and was about to say something when a young man carrying a basket filled with exotic flowers announced, "Kate O'Brien. Flowers for Kate O'Brien."

"Mom, that's us," Dee said excitedly before calling out, "Over here!"

The smiling young man brought the basket over to the table and set it down. "They were just delivered."

"Thank you," Kate said, bewildered by the gift. Who could have sent them? she wondered. They were lovely—a bright hibiscus surrounded by pale yellow-and-white orchids, carnations, and plumeria. Stuck in the middle of the fragrant arrangement was a card. Kate took it out and read aloud, "To Kate and Dee—have a beautiful vacation—from Hollis, Bella, and the rest of the gang at Annabella."

"Annabella?" George asked. "What, or who, is that?"

"It's a manicure salon in L.A.," Dee piped in. "Brentwood really. It's where my mom—"

"Gets her nails done," Kate interrupted smoothly, ignoring a surprised look from Dee.

It was the truth, sort of. Bella, one of the salon's owners, *had* done Kate's nails for her. What she was leaving out was the fact that she, Kate, worked at Annabella. She was a manicurist by profession, and she didn't want George to know it, not yet. People still tended to look down on manicurists. The old stereotype of gossipy, gum-chewing, lower-class women who didn't have the skills to do anything except apply nail polish still persisted.

It rankled, of course, because it was far from the truth. The women she worked with were bright and ambitious. But Kate had experienced that condescending attitude from several of her wealthier, more snobbish clients over the years, and she'd had to learn not to let it get to her. Still, she told herself, if she wanted the "right" kind of man, like George, for instance—he was a business and tax lawyer—she should probably not let him know what she did for a living. At least not at first.

It was only a little white lie, she told herself, but she felt uncomfortable nevertheless. Kate was nothing if not honest, and this bending of the truth niggled at her.

T. R. noted Kate's momentary discomfort and wondered what it was about. But he didn't spend a lot of energy wondering because he was too taken with how she looked. A lot of pretty young girls peaked as teenagers, then went downhill from there. Not Kate.

Without the sunglasses and hat she'd worn earlier, the Kate O'Brien of today was easier to compare to the one in his memory. Her hair was darker, more of a honey-blond now, with lighter streaks. She wore it loose, falling to her shoulders in soft waves. The eyes were the same—California-cheerleader-blue—but now he could see the fine lines around them. Her cheekbones were more pronounced, less rounded than before. She had on very little makeup, but it was subtle, probably expensive, and her lips, those full, pouting lips the boys used to make smart-ass cracks about, were painted a shiny coral color. They glistened, unintentionally inviting.

He licked his own lips as he followed the long line of her neck down to her dress. The bikini she'd been wearing earlier had pretty much told the story of all she had to offer, but the dress—it was more covered, but somehow sexier. The color gave a warm pink glow to her pale arms and chest, and the halter top fit like a second skin, the cotton outlining and molding her generous breasts. There was a deep shadowed cleft between them, and enough creamy flesh was exposed to make him shift in his seat and casually cross one of his knees over the other, so the sudden swelling in the front of his bathing suit would go undetected.

He watched her chatting with George, but it was obvious George wasn't her type. The guy was very straight, key of C, definitely. No sharps, no flats. No surprises. Somehow, T. R. knew Kate required surprises. If she gave him the opportunity, he would make sure she got them.

"The flower in the center should be worn in your hair," T. R. said to Kate.

"Really?"

"Yeah. It's a tradition, kind of. Lets people know that you're available."

"It does, does it?"

She didn't like that last bit about being available, he could tell. Chewing on her bottom lip, she looked at the hibiscus, then at him, then at George. She seemed unsure of herself, off balance for a brief moment. Then she shrugged, smiled, and plucked out the brilliant flower. There was a little comb attached to the stem, and Kate put it behind her ear. She turned to T. R., a sardonic look on her face, making fun of the tradition.

Then their eyes met, and he said, "Very nice."

Her expression became suddenly serious, and a little scared too. He could see a subtle blush just starting on her neck.

She felt that zing between them, no doubt about it. Man, were they going to be great together. She could fight it all she wanted, but she'd lose.

"Kate O'Brien," he said softly. "You should wear flowers all the time."

She looked down at her lap, still worrying her luscious lower lip with her teeth. She didn't like compliments, it seemed. His compliments, anyway. But she sure did look adorable when she blushed.

Adorable? he repeated silently. When was the last time he used that word?

"Well . . ." T. R. rose and stretched luxuriously. "I gotta go. I didn't mean to intrude."

Dee got up from her chair. "Me too."

"Dee, stay and visit with us," Kate said.

George, who had looked puzzled when he had arrived with the drinks to find a full table, now became expansive. "No, don't leave, Dee. Let me buy you a soda or something. And what about—T. R. is it?"

"It is."

George chuckled. "Maybe something more alcoholic for you?"

T. R. didn't bother saying that he no longer drank

anything stronger than the occasional beer. He'd cleaned up his act five years ago, after a decade of screwing around and losing himself in debauchery that had wasted—even killed—some of his musician friends. "No, it's okay. Thanks, anyway. I've got stuff to do. See you around."

And he was gone. *See you around.* Again. And again, Kate felt as if she'd lost something important. She wanted to call him back, but, of course, she didn't.

It wasn't fair. Two minutes in his presence, and she was distracted and ill at ease. She'd been having a perfectly good time discussing—What had she been talking about with George before T. R. and Dee came up? For the life of her, she couldn't remember.

George. She turned back to him, planting a bright smile on her face. "Dee is the reason we're here, George. She won this trip on a radio rock contest."

"Well, well, well. That's great. My son Tod listens to that kind of music too. In fact, he's in the room somewhere."

As George looked around for his son, Kate studied his face. Nothing there set off any sparks, in her at least. She tried to remind herself that she wasn't looking for sparks. That was in the past. She was looking for company and security.

She was thirty-three years old and the sole support of both her mother and her daughter. They lived in an old shabby house in Culver City, directly in the flight path of the nearby Los Angeles International Airport. It was a tough, tiring life; Kate often worked ten hours a day, and while she earned decent enough money, her mother's illness left none to spare.

Mostly Kate accepted her lot gracefully, even cheerfully. Between Mom and Dee and her friends at work, there was a lot of love and a lot of laughs. And they weren't starving or anything. But Mom's last bout in the hospital had eaten up the nest egg that Kate had saved over ten years—money for the down payment on a small condo, money for Dee's college education, that little extra "in case" money. Gone. How could she ever build up such a savings again?

She'd been going it alone for so long. Why not try to find a man who was reliable and solid, someone like George? Or if not him, someone else. As a lot of her clients were fond of saying, it was just as easy to love a wealthy man as a poor one.

But was it just as easy to love a steady bread-winner as a man who made music?

Three

After a delicious dinner of fresh fish, savory rice, and the ubiquitous pineapple, Kate settled herself in a big, flower-patterned easy chair and sighed contentedly, pleased to have some time to herself. Here, on the terrace that extended around the perimeter of the hotel, she was able to see firsthand one of the world-famous spectacular Hawaiian sunsets. A line of tall, graceful palm trees stood in relief against clouds of liquid gold and red and orange. Beyond the trees, the ocean reflected the blaze of colors like a rippling mirror. It was all, and more, than she'd heard it was.

Dee was on the beach with Tod and some of the other kids she'd met that day. George, who was sounding a bit like a broken record, talking about his ex-wife as though she were up for sainthood, was off somewhere. When Kate had told him that she needed some time alone, he'd gotten that hurt-puppy look on his face again.

She sighed. In her heart, she knew there was absolutely no attraction there, but she was reluctant to give up on him, not yet. The poor man was obviously having a hard time and required some tolerance on her part. Besides, she'd scouted the resort that afternoon, surreptitiously, of course, and there was a decided lack of mature, single men around the place; George was definitely the best bet.

"Beautiful, isn't it?"

She recognized T. R.'s soft, lilting tone of voice without looking around. "Seen one sunset, you've seen them all," she said lightly, to cover the sudden speeding up of her heart.

"Yeah. All that glorious color is boring, huh."

He was standing right behind her, but she didn't turn her head to look at him. "Ho-hum, I was just saying to myself."

He chuckled, a nice, rich sound, and knelt next to her, resting an elbow on the chair arm. He pointed off into the distance. "See those two peaks? They blow me away every time I look at them. Mauna Kea and further on, Mauna Loa."

"I was wondering about them. They're pretty tall, aren't they?"

"About thirteen thousand five hundred feet. They're volcanos."

"Seriously?"

"One dormant, one active. We're lucky we can see them tonight. Usually they're surrounded by clouds."

Kate finally turned in his direction. He was staring off at the volcanos, giving her a view of his profile. Strong and masculine, like the rest of him. Thick eyebrows. The sculpted line of his jaw defined by the shadows cast by the day's end. And generous, full lips, made for—

She swallowed and rested her chin on her hand. "You've been here a lot, I take it," she said. "In Hawaii, I mean."

Turning to her with a lazy smile, he said, "Yeah, I've played a lot of gigs in Oahu, Maui, singles bars, stuff like that. But this island is my favorite."

"Do you play alone? Like piano bar?"

"No way."

He got up from his crouching position and leaned back against a wooden support beam, facing her. The red-gold of the setting sun outlined his sturdily muscled silhouette. With his arms folded across his chest and his legs crossed at the ankles, he seemed both powerful and casual at the same time. He had changed into long cotton pants and a tight T-shirt that molded every curve, every line of his brawny torso.

"I play with a band," he said. "Or I used to. Let me see, I first came here over eighteen years ago. Yeah, right after I didn't graduate from high school."

"That must have been the last time you cut your hair."

"Why, Kate O'Brien, don't tell me you don't like long hair on men?"

She smiled slightly at his mocking tone as she regarded him. "Not on most, I admit. But somehow on you—" She left the thought unfinished.

"On me, what?"

She shrugged nonchalantly. "It looks good."

He bowed. "Thank you. That must be my Indian ancestry. And speaking of looking good, that goes double for you. You look better than good."

Their gazes locked for a moment, and she could feel the pull of those sapphire-blue eyes, which reflected the glow of the soft lighting around the porch. She shivered.

"Cold?" he asked.

She rubbed her bare arms. "Not really."

With a graceful, pantherlike move, he pushed himself away from the post. "Then how about a stroll along the beach?"

"I don't know. I'm kind of tired."

"You need a little exercise to revive you."

And suddenly he was bending down, loosening

the straps of her sandals. The touch of his fingers on her ankles sent tiny tremors up her leg.

"What are you doing?" she asked.

"Taking off your shoes. The sand feels terrific on bare feet." Slipping out of his moccasins, he put both pairs of shoes under the chair and reached for her hand. "Come on."

She didn't take his hand, but nevertheless, Kate found herself walking along a beach in Hawaii at sunset next to a man who practically reeked of musk, arousing such intense reactions in her mind and body, she could almost feel herself swooning like some Victorian heroine.

As they strolled for a while in silence, she told herself to cut it out. Her . . . primitive response to him was too strong, way out of line; she felt like a panting, sex-starved idiot. She was probably ovulating, and something about the tides or the smell of the flowers or the seething volcanoes was getting to her.

"I still can't get over running into you on the beach today," said T. R., obviously completely oblivious to Kate's current state of mind, for which she was truly thankful. "I mean, it isn't often that the object of your dreams shows up."

That got her attention. "Dreams? What dreams?"

"Old ones, for sure. You meant a lot to me back then." Shoving his hands in his pockets, he went on, "I was unhappy in school, and angry. My mother died when I was ten, and my dad drank a lot. I could never make friends because we moved so much and, I don't know, I guess I was pretty cynical. It was hard to get excited about much of anything then." He grinned. "Except girls, of course."

She grinned back, enjoying the slow, lazy rhythm of his voice and the sensation of cooling sand granules between her toes. "Of course."

"But you were special. You gave off a glow, you

had so much energy. You seemed to get such a kick out of life."

"I did, didn't I?" She shook her head ruefully. "High school is such a long time ago."

"But I never forgot you. Just being around you made me feel like maybe it wasn't all crap. Maybe there could be something worthwhile."

"It's so strange, knowing I had such an effect on someone and being completely unaware of it. I'm sorry I don't remember you," she said sincerely. "I really am."

He shrugged his shoulders. "It's okay. I had pimples and was kind of short—I didn't reach my height till I was twenty. And I tended to stay in corners and watch people."

"Still—"

"No big deal, I mean it. I loved to watch you. You were a knockout." He laughed. "No matter how much in the dumper I've been, I've always appreciated beautiful women."

"Come on, T. R. I wasn't a woman then. I was a girl."

"But now you're a woman." He slanted an approving look at her. "A beautiful woman. The years have been good to you, Kate," he said.

She expelled a soft sigh as his words washed over her. "Thank you. And now, may we change the subject?"

"Yeah, I noticed you don't like compliments."

"I've never been real comfortable with them. It's just that—" She stopped and looked out at the ocean. The darkening sky was fast erasing the line between the horizon and the oncoming night. Stars were beginning to glitter, and the twilight was peaceful and quiet, except for the soft rippling of waves at the shoreline and the twanging of a faraway steel guitar.

Kate kicked the sand at her feet and looked down, feeling unsure of herself. "It's hard to explain. Besides, I don't really know you."

He stood very close; she felt a pull between them, a magnet drawing her closer and closer.

"Try me anyway," he said quietly. "I catch on pretty quick."

She looked up from making patterns with her toes and met his gaze. His expression was kind, and she was struck suddenly with how *nice* he could be, and how surprised she was to discover this quality in him.

"I've never *felt* beautiful," she said hesitantly. "I could see in the mirror that I was . . . pretty, but that's all about genes and good health. And I know that being pretty has advantages, but it has disadvantages too. People don't take you seriously. They think you're dumb. More than anything, I wanted to get away from the blond bimbo image. I wanted to be taken seriously."

He nodded. "Yeah, I understand about that, believe me."

Their eyes locked. There was that connection again, Kate thought, that rapport between them that went beyond sexual attraction, a sense of sharing common emotional ground. She found herself wanting to tell him about how she had yearned for a college education and the chance to travel, that she had wanted to meet new, interesting people and do something important and worthwhile with her life, but instead had wound up becoming a teen-age mother and painting the nails of wealthy women, and that as each year slipped by, she wondered if she'd ever see any of her dreams come true.

But she didn't say any of that. Scared that she'd almost unburdened her innermost feelings, and scared of how drawn to this man she felt at this moment, she closed her eyes, afraid to look at him. Standing as close as he was, she could hear the sound of his breathing and imagined his warm breath on her bare skin.

"I think I'd like to go back to the hotel," she said. "I'm tired."

"I'm sorry," he said. "You just got in last night, didn't you? I forgot." He turned around, and they both headed back the way they'd come. "How long will you be here?"

"A week."

"Good. There's time to do some sight-seeing, then."

"Yes." Good, she told herself. They were back to small talk. "I plan to talk to the people at the front desk in the morning about a couple of day trips."

"No need," he said easily. "I'll be glad to take you and Dee around."

"Thanks, but I think I'd prefer a tour."

"Really?" Giving her a you're-putting-me-on look, he went on, "Being herded around on a bus with a lot of old ladies with blue hair? Stopping every five minutes at souvenir shops to buy hula skirts and postcards? You'd prefer that to being with me?"

She laughed, attracted to his sense of humor. Attracted to the man, to everything about him, if the truth be told. "I'm a sucker for souvenirs. I can't seem to get enough."

He shrugged. "Well then, I guess Dee will be disappointed."

"Dee?"

"I was telling her about Volcanoes National Park, and an early morning bike ride I took once around the crater of a live volcano. There's one particular spot where you can see the lava flowing into the ocean, and the beach is made of black sand. I thought we might go snorkeling one day, maybe pack a picnic and go into the rain forest on another. Stuff like that, stuff you don't get on tours. She seemed pretty enthusiastic."

Kate stopped walking and, folding her arms across her chest, looked at T. R. through narrowed eyes. "You're really doing this, aren't you?"

"Doing what?"

"Getting to me through my daughter."

" 'Getting to you'? What are you talking about?"

She almost applauded his expression of injured innocence. "Look, T. R.," she said firmly, then stopped puzzled. "What does that stand for again?"

"Tomás."

"Tomás," she repeated. "Do I call you Tomás or Tom or what?"

He wiggled his eyebrows. "Call me whatever you want, just call me."

She tried to suppress the giggle that suddenly rose in her throat, but couldn't. "Stop it," she said, her mouth twitching. "Do you hear me? I don't want to enjoy myself with you."

"Why not?"

She threw her hands up in exasperation. "Because you're a musician. A rock musician. Do you understand? You're my worst nightmare. You're bad news. You're poison."

"You left out the black death." Shaking his head, he put his hands on his hips and stared at her. "Come on, Kate, how can I be all those things when you know nothing at all about me?"

Once again crossing her arms over her chest, she announced, "I know all I need to know, believe me."

"Do you? Tell me all about me," he challenged.

"Okay. You eat, breathe, and live music. You have an interior rhythm—whenever there's a beat, it's like your heart keeps time with it. You love nighttime, you love nightlife. You probably drink too much, maybe do dope. You can zero in on a woman making eyes at you from a hundred yards away, even with a spotlight in your eyes."

She had begun her speech, ticking off each item on her fingers, in the spirit of picking up the gauntlet T. R. had thrown down. But as she went on, she could feel herself getting passionately caught up in what she was saying.

"You sometimes remember to pay your bills," she continued, "you get restless if you're in one place too long, and you like women fine—when you want one—but you'd prefer it if they didn't talk too much. You're lazy. You don't read the newspaper, or vote, or give much of a damn about anything except the sounds in your head or the sounds you make with other musicians. And most of all, you leave. You always leave."

After snapping out these final words, Kate put her hand over her mouth, feeling herself perilously close to tears. She was horrified, both at the scope of the list she'd just made and, equally, at the extent of her own pain and how she'd let it show.

What was it about this man that made her want to share her deepest feelings? How could she put a stop to the river of intimacy that kept flowing from her toward him? Hugging herself, she turned and looked out to sea.

Some of what Kate said had been on the money, at least in the past, but oddly enough, T. R. didn't feel criticized by her. What he felt—and was surprised to feel—instead, was compassion. There was a lot of sadness behind that lovely blond, blue-eyed exterior, that wisecracking facade. But he knew instinctively that this wasn't the time to explore her innermost feelings.

He also didn't feel like exploring his own mixed reactions to her outpouring—an overwhelming tenderness, a yearning to hold her and take care of her. What had happened to his goal of an old-fashioned conquest? What were all these other, softer emotions that were now in the way? The whole thing was damned unsettling.

A lock of her hair had fallen in front of her eyes, and he reached over and pushed it behind her ear.

She thrust his hand aside. "Don't."

She turned away and walked toward the hotel, her head bent. Following, he let a little time go by before he spoke. "Man, I got to say, I've never been so thoroughly pigeonholed in my life."

"I'm sorry, really I am," she muttered. "I was out of line."

"Not really. Some of it's right on, of course, but not all of it. For instance," he said lightly, "I *do* read the newspaper. Every day, as a matter of fact. I like to do the crossword puzzle."

He could sense her waiting for him to continue, but he just kept trudging on through the sand with her.

She was the one to break the silence. "That's it? That's all you're going to say?"

"What else would you like me to say?"

"I thought you'd at least want to tell me how you're not like other musicians. I assume there are exceptions. I thought you'd want to defend yourself."

"No, I don't particularly want to defend myself," he said easily. "I am who I am, and I like my life just fine."

"But—" She looked at him, puzzled, even a little disappointed. Then she expelled a breath. "So, that's it, then."

He shrugged. "Guess so."

When they reached the veranda, he knelt down and retrieved her sandals. "Shall I put them on for you?"

"That won't be necessary, thank you," she said coolly, taking them from him. "I learned to buckle my own shoes a long time ago."

"I'll just bet you did."

She was as closed up as she could be, T. R. observed, like a turtle who had stuck its head out briefly and then retreated back into the solid safety of the shell.

"You should probably soak up the sun again tomorrow," he advised. "Let's do the volcano trip the day after. Plan on leaving pretty early, before sunrise."

She looked confused. In the flickering light from candles placed all around the veranda, her face was imbued with a soft, romantic glow. "Didn't you hear me?" she said. "I thought I made myself pretty clear. I don't think it's a good idea for us to see each other."

"That may be, but it's all arranged. I've invited Dee and your friend George and his son, Tod, along too. They seem to want to be with me, even if you don't."

"You've been busy, haven't you?"

"Amazing, huh. Sometimes we lazy musicians actually get off our butts and plan ahead."

Kate honestly didn't know how to react to this man. She'd told him to back off, in no uncertain terms, and her firm rejection would have sent most men running for the hills. But not T. R. He seemed impervious to her negative attitude toward him, brushing it off like he would a pesky fly.

"Why?" she asked.

"Why what?"

"Why are you going to all this trouble?"

The smoldering look in his eyes gave her the answer before his words did. "I like you, in case you haven't noticed. I also want you."

She let out a big, shuddering breath, suddenly afraid, not of him, but of herself. "You're honest, I'll say that much. It's just that I don't want you."

"Sure you do."

One long, graceful finger brushed her cheek, and slowly, tantalizingly, traced her suddenly heated skin—over her cheekbone, around the jaw, along her chin, down the length of her neck, and back and forth over her collarbone. Everywhere he touched he left an exquisite tingling sensation in his wake.

"You're just having a little war with yourself," he murmured.

"My war is with you," she managed, suddenly finding it difficult to breathe. She could feel her nipples harden with the need for his teasing finger to dip lower, lower. "And, believe me, you won't be the winner."

He raised his hand to her mouth and lightly ran the pad of his thumb across the generous flesh of her lower lip. Then he brought his thumb up to his own mouth and licked it slowly, his tongue taking all the time in the world to savor the taste of her.

All the while he stared at her, pinning her with his intense blue eyes. "Won't I?"

He waited a heartbeat, lifted the corners of his mouth in a slight, knowing smile, and walked off into the night.

"Come *on*, Mom, we'll be late!"

"I'm moving as fast as I can, honey. You go on ahead." Kate yawned as she dragged along the corridor toward the hotel lobby, envying her daughter's perkiness, her ability to wake up and feel human right away. But it was four-thirty in the morning, for God's sake. How could she, Kate, be expected to move quickly, much less be upright and conscious, in the middle of the night?

They were on their way to take a sunrise bike ride around a volcano. George had invited, and Dee had begged, and Kate had finally given in. T. R. had done a great job getting everyone hyped about the excursion.

And when she thought about it, Kate decided that she was being silly in fighting him so hard. She'd obviously overreacted to him that first night on the beach, probably due to a combination of moonlight and jet lag.

What she felt toward T. R., she told herself firmly, was nothing more than a hormonal response—one that didn't have to be acted on—and it was foolish to let that prevent her from seeing the sights, maybe actually enjoying herself. If she allowed him to get to her that way, then she'd learned nothing from the past. She would put the whole thing in perspective.

Just to be safe, however, she would be sure to stick close to George today.

When she got to the lobby, T. R., Dee, and Tod were there, but not George.

"Dad's not coming," Tod said, looking rumpled and apologetic. His hair was the same color as his father's and he also wore glasses, but he wasn't yet as tall as George—or even as tall as Dee. "He was in the sun too much yesterday, and he's running a fever. The doctor says he has to stay in bed for a couple of days."

"Bummer," said Dee. "We'll bring something back for him, all right, Mom?"

Kate nodded absently, her reaction a mixture of compassion and irritation. Without George along as a buffer, she'd find it more difficult to dismiss T. R. today.

As soon as they got into the four-wheel drive, she moved as far from T. R. as she could, pressing her body tight against the passenger door. As the Jeep bounced along, she tried looking out the window, but it was still dark outside, so all Kate could make out was the occasional tall palm tree caught in the glare of headlights, and moonlight reflected on green leafy trees, lots of them. She closed her eyes, letting the conversation between T. R. and his youthful backseat passengers lull her to sleep.

"Wake up, sleepyhead," T. R. said after what seemed like only seconds. "We're here."

Kate shook her head as she opened her eyes. How long had she been out? she wondered as T. R. swung the Jeep into a parking lot about halfway up what looked like a very tall mountain. The sky was just beginning to lighten as the other three hopped out to unload the bikes from the rear bike rack. Kate moved more slowly, wishing she were more of a morning person.

"Come *on*, Mom," Dee urged.

"Working on it, honey." She couldn't seem to stop yawning.

When they got on their bikes, Kate's muscles protested. It had been years since she'd done this. But after a few wobbly turns around the parking lot, her body adjusted, and she smiled for the first time that morning. This was actually fun.

As they rode their bikes up the mountain—walking them in the steeper sections—T. R. became their tour guide. "The Big Island is less than a million years old, which is pretty young. And with all the volcanic activity, it's still forming. I think it adds about a hundred new acres every ten years, or something like that."

"Neat," Dee said, pedaling so that she was riding abreast of T. R. "Can we touch the lava?"

"Not a good idea. It'll burn you to a crisp. But it's fun to walk around knowing there's all this commotion right under your feet."

"Is it dangerous?" Tod asked, coming up on T. R.'s other side, leaving Kate contentedly bringing up the rear where she found her attention drawn to the way the muscles in T. R.'s buttocks, outlined nicely in his skintight biking pants, bunched and expanded as he pedaled.

"Not really," T. R. said. "They've got the dangerous sections roped off. If you stay outside the fence, you'll be okay."

As they rode higher along the path to the summit, the predawn light revealed bare tree branches and black sand. Nothing green survived the path of the lava.

"This looks like a set for a slasher flick," Dee observed.

"Cool," Tod said approvingly.

It *was* cool, chilly actually, and Kate was glad they'd worn windbreakers. She was also glad they'd reached more level ground—she was about out of breath. Not the other three, of course—two youngsters in their prime and a man with thighs so well developed that he could probably acquit himself admirably in the Tour de France.

Don't think about his thighs, Kate told herself. Concentrate on the scenery.

The four of them pretty much had the road to themselves, and the sun rose as they pedaled, but as they were so high, it rose below them—a strange, oddly affecting sight, Kate thought, feeling as though she had been let in on a secret. Streams of light poured into the morning sky as they rode along the rim of the Kilauea Crater. All around them, the lava-encrusted landscape was black and barren, yet beautiful. At the summit they parked the bikes and looked down into the two-mile-wide crater. Steam and sulfurous fumes rose from hundreds of fissures in the floor.

It was a fascinating sight; Kate imagined the beginning of the earth might have looked something like this. The altitude must have had an effect, because she was suddenly swept with a sense of power, of indomitability. If she jumped off the edge of the earth, she imagined she would fly.

As she looked around to see if anyone else was experiencing what she was, Kate was aware of T. R. coming up just behind her.

"Good morning," he said softly, making the back of her neck tingle. "Having a good time?"

"Yes, it's wonderful, like nothing else," she replied honestly. "I'm glad I let you talk me into it."

"I thought you'd feel like that."

She smiled. "Don't be smug."

"Sorry. It just slipped out."

"The morning would be perfect if you had a cup of coffee on you." She angled her head to look up at him and blinked slowly. "I don't suppose you do?"

"Sorry. Look out at what's around us. That'll wake you up."

Turning back to the view, Kate breathed deeply, aware that standing on top of a volcano, she felt a sense of unpredictability, risk, a subtle danger.

Standing close to T. R. aroused the same sense of danger. The gray morning clouds and mist were melting gradually in the heat of the sun. T. R. gave off heat, too, the kind that was difficult to ignore. With him this close, his presence was unnerving; Kate thought about moving away from him, nearer to Dee, maybe. But her body seemed unwilling to make the effort.

"Feel it?" he said.

"Feel what?"

He placed his hands on her shoulders, lightly and caressingly, causing her breath to stop. "The lava," he said in a low, intimate voice. "It lies just beneath the surface, hot and bubbling, straining to get free."

He paused, then whispered in her ear, "If you stand very still and close your eyes, you can sense the mountain moving."

Kate swallowed and closed her eyes, hypnotized by the sound of his voice, his warm breath on her neck, his hands on her shoulders, the sense of restlessness in the ground beneath her feet . . . and her own rapidly beating heart.

Time stopped for a long moment. The sun climbed higher in the sky. A flock of native geese flew overhead.

She sighed. "Yes. I feel it."

"Good," he said in a throaty whisper.

"Where's the lava, T. R.?" Dee asked. "All we see is steam."

Her daughter's question broke the spell, and Kate opened her eyes. Back to earth. Back to regular heartbeats. Back to breathing. She took a few steps out from under T. R.'s touch and his spell, taking care to avoid his eyes.

"The lava's running down the side, then into the sea," he replied. "You'll see it better down below. Come on."

He led them around the rim of the crater, then through a small, lush fern forest. Finally they reached the Volcano House restaurant, which was serving a large buffet breakfast.

While the two young people ate heartily, T. R. pushed some eggs around on his plate, keeping an eye on Kate, trying to assess her mood. Or moods. She'd been through a few of them already, and it wasn't even noon yet. She'd held him at arm's length most of the morning, but he'd gotten to her up there at the crater, he knew it. Right now, she was paying a lot of attention to her coffee cup and the conversation of the teenagers, doing her best to shut him out.

He hated feeling like an outsider—it was too familiar a role in his life.

"They're, like, so hot!" Dee said to Tod, extolling the virtues of her new favorite band.

"I've never heard of them," Tod said apologetically.

After a pitying look at him, Dee turned to T. R. "You have, haven't you?"

He nodded. "They're pretty good. The bass player's the whole sound."

"See?" Dee turned back to Tod. "T. R. says they're hot too."

He moved his chair closer to Kate. "Dee knows her stuff, doesn't she?" he said. "She seems to be quite a fan."

"I wish she were just a fan. It's her life."

"Does she play an instrument?"

"A little guitar. Mostly she sings. She and her friends have a band—they play for dances."

"It's a calling, for sure," he said, smiling at Dee's animated face as the youngster discussed music. "If it's in your blood, there's not much you can do about it."

"That's what terrifies me," Kate said.

"Why?"

"I want a better life for her than that."

"Why are you so sure the life of a musician is such a bad one?"

"Magazine articles, drug and alcohol death statistics, word of mouth . . . personal experience." She drained her cup and looked around.

For a moment he wanted to offer a rebuttal of some sort. But he was pretty sure it would fall on deaf ears, and he didn't want the gulf between them to stretch any wider than it was. He decided to let it drop. "More coffee?"

"I'm not fit till I've had at least three."

T. R. signaled the waitress, all the time wondering if Kate even knew why she was fighting him so hard.

Why in the world was she fighting him so hard? Kate asked herself, not for the first time that morning. It wasn't his fault Dee loved music. It wasn't even his fault that, sitting here with him, she was feeling decidedly restless instead of carefree, as you were supposed to feel on a vacation. She knew what that restlessness meant, of course, but she was back to being of two minds about what to do. T. R. probably thought a roll in the hay would fix it, but she didn't think it was quite that simple. There were emotions involved. For her, at least.

She supposed she was drawn to him because he was bad for her. How many more times was she fated to make the same mistake?

After breakfast, T. R. took them on a mile-long hike along the newly hardened ash-colored lava toward the edge of the ocean. As steam rose up from the earth and surrounded their legs, Kate watched, smiling, as Dee and Tod squealed energetically and danced around. With every few steps, the burning became more intense.

Soon they were near the water's edge and there she stared in fascination as the bubbling orange lava emerged from miles of underground travel, plopped into the ocean, and then sizzled as it met the cool water. A cloud of steam extended into the sky for miles, as high, it seemed to Kate, as the mountain behind them.

It was terribly exciting, thrilling, really. All that energy, all that heat, all that chaos, she thought with wonder—nature at her most lavishly unpredictable. Dee must have been feeling the same way because she laughed joyously and put her arms around Kate. "This is so neat, Mom!" she exclaimed. "I'm so glad we did this."

"So am I, honey," Kate said, returning the hug enthusiastically. "So am I."

As they all watched the huge white plume rising into the atmosphere, T. R. had to shout to be heard over the noise, even though he was right beside them. "They say the steam represents a battle between the two greatest deities in Hawaiian mythology—Pele, the goddess of fire, and her sister, Namaka, the goddess of the sea."

He moved a little closer to Kate and grinned.

"Just goes to show what can happen when two equally strong forces collide," he said. "All that heat, all that steam. It can get pretty exciting."

Kate met his gaze. Lifting an eyebrow sardonically, she said, "Some might call it exciting. Others might call it a catastrophe. I guess it depends on your point of view."

"What's your point of view?" he challenged.

"When I know, you'll be the first one I'll tell."

"Is that a promise?"

"Cross my heart."

His vivid blue eyes locked on hers for a moment longer, then he began to laugh—a hearty laugh that she hadn't heard from him previously. It was irresistible. Kate joined in. Soon the kids were laughing, too, their sounds of happiness merging with the rising steam as it sailed into the heavens.

Four

They were on a pristine white beach under an azure cloudless sky. No one else was around. T. R. came toward her with a slow yet persistent stride. He had that smug smile on his face, the one that said, "Come on, you know you want me." She tried to move back, away from him, but her feet seemed to be stuck in the spot where she stood. Her heartbeat sped up. She could hear the echo of it pounding in her ears as, helpless, she watched him drawing closer and closer. Then he was facing her, a half inch of air separating them.

She was nude, so was he. She could hear his labored breathing as it mingled with hers. With his palm, he cupped her cheek, then moved his hand down over her neck and chest. He brought his other hand up and covered both breasts, squeezing them gently, molding them, sighing with pleasure. Or was it her own sighs she was hearing? His long index fingers made teasing circles all around the tender flesh of her breasts, the circles getting smaller and smaller, until he was outlining but not touching the *aureoles. A deep, shuddering breath escaped her at this slow, excruciatingly light movement toward her nipple.*

He was playing with her, taking his own sweet time, because he knew she wasn't going to stop him. She had stopped fighting and had given him all the power.

She was scared.

She was exhilarated.

Her skin flushed with fever as she arched her back, begging him to touch her aching, throbbing nipple.

He laughed and murmured, "Kate."

She groaned. From somewhere behind her on the beach, a knocking sound was heard.

"Kate," he said again, louder this time.

She opened her eyes. Her own hands lay on her breasts. She looked around the room, totally disoriented. She was lying in her bed, alone.

It had been a dream.

"Kate!" T. R.'s voice cut through her consciousness again. It was coming from the other side of the hotel room door.

"Just a minute," she called out, her voice hoarse with morning. Looking around for something to put on, her gaze fell on a colorful muumuu she'd bought in Hilo yesterday; it was sticking out of a bag and still had the price tag on it. She swung her legs over the side of the bed, stretched briefly, and threw the garment over her head. As she made her way toward the door, she noted in the mirror above the dresser that she looked as tired and rumpled as she felt.

When she got to the door, she said, "What is it?"

"It's T. R. I have a message from Dee."

Kate opened the door a crack and peered out. "Dee? Is anything wrong?"

"Nothing's wrong."

He stood there, one arm resting casually against the wall, the other hand on his hip. He wore olive-green shorts and a matching sleeveless, scooped-neck T-shirt. His muscles bulged, his skin looked like bronze silk, his jet-black hair hung loose around his shoulders, and his eyes peered at her with amusement. He looked gorgeous.

"I think I got you out of bed," he said.

As she tried to bring her brain into focus, her dream came back to her with a wave of embarrassment. She crossed her arms and looked down at her toes. "You think right," she mumbled sleepily. "What did Dee say?"

"Aren't you going to invite me in?"

"I hadn't planned on it."

"Why? Afraid to have a man in your room?"

She leaned her head on the doorframe. "It's too early to fence, T. R. I'm not a morning person, remember? Besides, I look awful."

"No you don't. You look cute."

She arched an eyebrow at him. "Cute?"

"And cuddly. Can I come in now?"

She wrinkled her nose. "But I haven't even brushed my teeth yet."

Pushing the door open, he sauntered past her and over to the large picture windows across the room. "I can handle it."

She followed him with her eyes, not too tired to appreciate the way his snug shorts fit over his tight, muscular buttocks. She sighed. She didn't ever remember ogling a man as much as she had T. R. in the brief time she'd known him. Was it a sign of age or desperation?

"What did Dee say?"

He parted the curtains and peered out her window. "Nice view—you got a primo room."

"It was part of the deal. What did Dee say?"

"She and some of the kids are going surfing at a nearby beach. She said not to worry, she would be careful, and she'd see you this evening. She also said that Hawaii is both neat and cool, although not in the same sentence." He turned back toward her. "I think that's it."

Yawning, Kate put her hand over her mouth. "Why didn't she tell me herself?"

He folded his arms over his chest and leaned against the wall. "She said you're impossible to wake up in the morning. I said I'd be glad to give it a try."

"It's probably one of your specialties."

"No one's complained yet."

"You could have used the phone."

He grinned. "I'm an in-person kind of guy."

Kate fought down a smile. "Thanks for the message," she said. "I'll walk you to the door."

"But I don't want to leave just yet."

She clasped her hands under her chin imploringly. "T. R., have mercy on me," she pleaded. "I haven't even had a cup of coffee yet."

As if on cue, there was a knock on the open door, followed by a waiter with a tray bearing a carafe, two mugs, a basket of sweet rolls, and a bowl of fruit. He set it down on the rattan table near the window.

Kate frowned at the tray. "I didn't order that."

"No, I did."

She looked up from the table to T. R., who shrugged.

"Got to get you up and out," he said by way of explanation.

As he tipped the waiter and closed the door behind him, Kate said, "Why?"

T. R. poured coffee into one of the mugs and handed it to her. "Go on. Wash your face, brush your teeth, and put on one of those tiny little things you call a bathing suit. The tinier the better." Pouring a cup for himself, he sat down in a wide, cane-backed chair and settled comfortably into the cushion. "I'll wait right here."

She sipped the hot brown brew. It tasted delicious. "I'd rather go back to bed."

"Is that an invitation?"

"Absolutely not."

"Then you can nap this afternoon," he said cheerfully. "We can't waste the morning—it's the perfect time of day."

"For what?" Kate said.

"Snorkeling. Have you ever done it?"

"Years ago."

"I have all the equipment in the truck. There's a great stretch of beach a couple of miles down the road."

Kate set her coffee cup down and put her hands on her hips. "You're doing it again."

"What?"

"Manipulating me, telling me what to do. And I really hate being manipulated and told what to do."

"Gee," he said with a look of total innocence, "so do I. See how much we have in common?"

She found herself laughing and shaking her head. "You're not going to give up, are you?"

He looked at her over the rim of his cup. "We'd both hate it if I did."

She met his knowing, amused gaze, and thought that he was probably right, and then shook her head again, amazed she'd admitted that to herself.

"I have to shower first," she said.

"Why bother? You're going right into the water."

"After coffee, I shower. That's the ritual."

"Got it." He leaned back in the chair and closed his eyes. "I'll be right here."

Grabbing her cup, Kate went into the bathroom, careful to lock the door behind her. Under the shower, she found herself humming a tune that she soon identified as an old Simon and Garfunkel ode to "feelin' groovy." She grinned and lifted her face into the hot spray.

Yes, indeed, she thought as she lathered herself all over with the almond-scented soap bar provided by the hotel, there was a definite change in the mood between her and T. R. It had taken a turn for the lighter.

The difference was with her, not him. She had decided to stop equivocating about the attraction between them and to confront it with as much honesty as she could. She was on vacation, for heaven's sake, and T. R. made her laugh. It had been a long time since an attractive, available man had made her laugh.

She'd been dreaming about him every night, pretty steamy dreams, if what she remembered of this morning's little example was any hint. It was time to stop stressing out, as Dee would say. T. R. was available; so was she. In the absense of any solid husband-type candidates—George was definitely in the noncontender category—Kate would allow herself a mild flirtation, a vacation fling.

If she'd entertained the thought that her feelings were in danger of running deeper than that, it was because she'd fallen under the proverbial spell of the tropics. There would be no big romance, no talk of love, no heavy complications. She'd make sure of it. And in a few days, both of them would be back to their separate realities. She and Dee would return to L.A., and T. R. would return to—

Kate stood still for a moment, letting the scented steam surround her. Where did he live? she wondered. Probably in a suitcase, like most musicians. She knew precious little about him, actually. She'd kept their conversation superficial on purpose. Well, there was nothing wrong with a little *Q* and *A*. And she'd tell him a little about herself too. Why not?

She smiled, luxuriating as the shower's hot needles rinsed away the last of her morning grumpiness. Fighting her attraction to T. R. had interfered with over half of her precious Hawaiian vacation so far. Giving up the fight, she no longer perceived any barrier to "having a wonderful time," as the postcards always said.

T. R. sat contentedly, his eyes closed, thinking what a lot of fun Kate was when she wasn't doing her hands-off routine. He tried to remember when—if ever—he'd been with a woman who intrigued him, moved him, engaged him, made him laugh, the way this one did. The answer was never.

Listening to the sound of her shower, he gave himself over to imagining her body. He knew what it looked like already, except for the most intimate parts; he and she would fit together beautifully. Picturing her now with slick droplets of water clinging to pale golden skin, he felt himself get hard, as he had many times in the past few days when he thought about her.

The sound of the shower stopped. He kept his eyes closed. Now she was stepping out of the stall and rubbing herself all over with a thick terry cloth towel, over her back, her breasts, down and up her long legs, to the curly thatch between her thighs.

He groaned, enjoying the fantasy, but finding his groin painful with wanting her.

She hummed a little melody as she ran the sink faucet, probably brushing her teeth. She had a sweet voice, he noted, and could carry a tune, thank God. It would be difficult for him, a musician, to spend much time in the company of a woman who was tone-deaf.

The water was turned off. After a moment, the bathroom door opened. With his lids still lowered, he conjured up a vision of Kate completely nude, fresh from her shower and smelling of sweet soap and warm woman. She would pose for him briefly in the doorway, then throw herself into his arms. Every man's fantasy come to life.

"Where do you live?" Kate said.

He opened his eyes. Her hair was wrapped in a towel, and she had the muumuu on, completely covered as she rummaged in a drawer. So much for that fantasy. "Excuse me?"

"It occurred to me that I know next to nothing about you. Stuff like where you live, what kind of food you like to eat, you know, pertinent information."

"Sure you don't want to know my sign?" he drawled.

"Spare me."

He chuckled. "I'm on the road a lot, but I live officially in Montana."

She turned around and looked at him, her face registering surprise. Shiny and freshly scrubbed from her shower, she looked eighteen years old. He'd meant it when he'd said she looked cute.

"Montana? You don't seem like the type."

"What type is that?"

She thought for a moment. "Actually, I have no idea. Something to do with bowlegs and Stetsons, I guess."

"We have those in Montana." He shrugged. "I have a little place in the hills."

Several thousand acres, actually, he amended to himself, as she turned back to the pile of clothing sticking out of the drawer. But he was still determined not to let Kate know how successful he was. Time for that later—maybe a little postlovemaking pillow talk.

"What are you looking for in there?" he asked, changing the subject.

"I'm trying to decide which bathing suit to wear."

"Why don't you model all of them for me and I'll decide."

"I love it when you're subtle."

He grinned again. Damn, it felt good being with this lively, sexy woman. He couldn't remember when he'd ever enjoyed just bantering like this, feeling . . . playful, was the best way to describe it. Young again and unbruised by life. "How about you? Where in L.A. do you live?"

"Would you believe the same place I lived back in high school?"

"Actually, no. Where do you live, really?"

She pulled the towel off her head and, looking

into the mirror over the dresser, fluffed her hair out. "I just told you, good old Culver City. Dee and I live with my mom."

If she'd announced that she was a martian, she couldn't have said anything more surprising. The same place? A small wood-frame house in Culver City—he remembered walking by it all those years ago. The neighborhood had been lower-middle class back then, and as far as he knew hadn't enjoyed a revival in the intervening years.

Kate met his eyes in the mirror. "You look shocked."

"That's because I am," he said honestly. "This room, your clothes. I pictured, I don't know, Bel Air, Beverly Hills, Hancock Park."

"The airfare and deluxe room are compliments of a radio contest," she said dryly, turning around and resting a hip against the dresser. "The clothes are borrowed from a very rich, very nice woman I know, a customer of mine. I'm a manicurist, T. R. I have been since Dee was an infant."

He leaned back in his chair and shook his head ruefully. "So much for snap judgments. This is blowing me away. Here I thought you were one of those ladies who lunch and redecorate their houses every year."

She nodded. "You're describing about three quarters of my clients. Annabella is pretty upscale. But I'm not."

"Wow."

"What does 'Wow' mean?" Kate could hear a bit of defensiveness creeping into her voice and made herself take a deep breath. She had nothing to be ashamed of.

"It means that I was attracted to you in spite of what I thought you were, and that now that I know you are not what I thought you were, I am still attracted to you, maybe more so, and very glad that you are not what I thought you were." T. R. smiled. "Does that make sense?"

"Not in the least," she said, as something tense inside her relaxed.

In the ensuing moments neither of them spoke. But as they continued looking at each other, she could feel the mood in the room shift subtly, become more intimate somehow; there was less air now. T. R. leaned forward in his chair and rested his elbows on his knees. "Kate O'Brien," he said softly.

"What?" she replied, suddenly breathless.

"I can't believe I've spent this much time alone with you in this room without touching you."

She tried to think of something clever to say, but her powers of speech had dried up at the sound of his seductive, lilting voice. He stood and came toward her; she could feel all the magnetism and power of the man concentrated on her, spreading its enveloping heat over every inch of her. When he reached her, he stood very close, his blazing blue eyes warm and sexy. He sifted his fingertips through her still-wet hair, combing the silken strands back off her face, his touch a gentle caress.

"I like you, Kate O'Brien," he murmured, "and I like that you work for a living and that you are in touch with the reality of daily life, and are not insulated behind a wall of money and privilege."

Even as her body reacted meltingly to his touch, she searched his eyes questioningly. "Who are you, T. R.?"

He continued to stroke her hair as his gaze moved all over her face, lovingly examining each part of it. "Hmm?"

"One moment you sound like you don't have a serious thought in your head, and then you say something that makes you sound like a teacher or . . . a philosopher. Who are you?" she repeated.

"Good question. Maybe one day I'll tell you." He cupped her face in his hands. *"Querida,"* he whispered, and brought his mouth down to hers for a kiss.

It was a getting-to-know-you kiss. His lips were firm and soft at the same time and, with a sigh, Kate gave herself up to the enjoyment of him. He slid his mouth over hers, ever so delicately, his breath warm, as his palms on her cheeks held her still for his gentle assault.

Shuddering, she raised her arms to hug him, the firm muscles of his back feeling smooth and taut under her hands. It felt so good to touch him! She had wanted this closeness, this connection with him, from the first, and she no longer had to fight it.

She could hear her own groan as his kiss deepened. His tongue slid around her mouth, seeking further access to her. She parted her lips and let him in, aware of the tang of her toothpaste on his tongue, of the musky smell and taste of him, and of the way both of their breathing rates accelerated at the same time.

T. R. gripped Kate's hands and brought them up around his neck so that he could clasp her closer to him. He had an almost desperate need to make contact with every inch of her body. Changing the angle of his kiss so that he could taste more of her, he ran his hands up and down her back, over her hips, finally grasping her buttocks and pulling her up against his hard, aching flesh. She wore nothing under the muumuu, and he could feel the points of her hardened nipples against his chest. He groaned at the exploration of her fingers through his hair, her nails combing its thickness, those restless hands telegraphing the heat building inside her.

"*Querida*. Kate. Oh, baby." He kissed her neck, feeling her arch away from him to grant him more access. His feverish hands came around to the front of her, covering and massaging her breasts through the cotton fabric. The feel of the firm yet generous mounds, their stiff buds stabbing at the flesh of his palms, sent his senses into a reeling universe that was all touch and sensation, all heat and raging, rampaging sensuality.

The phone rang. It seemed to come from a long distance away. He ignored it.

"T. R.," Kate said.

Groaning again, he pressed his lips against the rapidly beating pulse at the base of her neck. Her skin was incredibly soft, smooth as powdered porcelain.

The phone rang again.

"T. R.," she said once more, pushing him away. "I need to answer that."

"Ignore it," he growled.

"I can't." She ducked under his arm and crossed to the bedside phone. "It might be important," she said, picking up the receiver. "Hello?"

She sounded as out of breath as he felt. He cursed with frustration, but then admonished himself to be patient. It was a temporary interruption, at worst.

Kate splayed her palm across her chest, as though trying to slow down her breathing. "Oh, hi, Mom. Anything wrong?" She listened for a while, then nodded, obviously relieved to find her mother was all right. "Yes, it's lovely. . . . No, no problem, I just got out of the shower, that's why I'm breathing so hard." She made a face at T. R., and he grinned back. She turned away from him as she continued talking to her mother.

So, she thought she could ignore him, did she? T. R. came up behind her and kissed her neck. She shrugged her shoulders in an attempt to make him stop, but he could tell that she was laughing too.

"Yes," she went on as he moved his body closer to hers, "we've been quite busy. We went to see a volcano the other day."

His hands snaked around her waist until he placed them flat on her stomach, pulling her tight against him.

She gasped. "Dee is having a great time . . . yes,

the clothes are perfect." Kate tried to dislodge his hands, but she was no match for his strength. She gave up trying and sank back into him, stroking the knuckles of his hand with her palm. "I'm so glad you're all right. I love you too, Mom. Give Aunt Tress a big kiss."

After she replaced the receiver, she turned into him, laying her head against his chest. "You shouldn't do that to a person when they're on the phone."

"I'm sorry," he said, nuzzling her neck once again. "Everything okay at home?"

"Umm-hmm. Mom has emphysema, so I always get a little panicked when the phone rings."

"I understand," he said, licking around her ear and enjoying the way she squirmed against him. "Now, where were we?"

With a small chuckle Kate pushed him away. "Going snorkeling, I was led to believe. Come on, music man, let's hit it."

Kate looked out over the rolling lawn of the hotel where the staff was cleaning up after a big twilight luau for the guests. There had been roast pig that had been cooked all day in the ground, hula dancers, music, leis for everyone—all the usual tourist stuff. But she'd loved it, every corny moment of it. Just as she'd loved her whole time in Hawaii.

She leaned back in her chair and sighed. "Poor me."

In the lounge next to hers, T. R. turned his head so he was looking at her. "Why poor you?"

"This is my last night, and I don't want to leave."

"Then don't."

"I have to. The contest paid for this week and no more. Besides, I have to get back to work. But I think I'll indulge in a little more self-pity." She sighed again. "Poor me."

Like picture postcards, images of the days spent

on the Big Island came to mind. Snorkeling amid a wonderland of lava tubes, coral and sponge formations. A huge turtle lumbering by, followed by schools of tropical fish in wild combinations of brilliant colors.

Hidden waterfalls that plummeted from impossible heights in lush rain forests. Kissing T. R. under a small cascade of warm water that pooled around their feet.

Brightly colored parrots. Coconuts. Dee waving as she rode an enormous wave. White clouds, glistening beaches, sailboats, kites flying in the wind. Golden sunsets brimming out of the sky.

She and T. R. laughing and playing in the water like two kids. Having trouble finding time alone with each other, but when they did, kissing and touching some more.

But not taking it any further, even though she burned with wanting him.

"Why?" he said, bringing her back to the present.

"Why what?"

"Why haven't we made love?"

He'd been reading her mind again. From the moment she'd stopped fighting him, they had seemed to be in sync with each other, like two people who had known each other for years instead of days. "I . . . I'm not quite sure."

"Take a stab at it," he said dryly.

"It's difficult with Dee around."

"She's been busy with all the kids she's met on the beach. We hardly ever see her."

"But she needs to know where I am anyway," Kate responded. "And I can't just say I'm going off with you and can't be disturbed—it sends a message that I'm not sure I want to send."

"What, that her mother has a life of her own?"

"She knows that already, T. R. No, it's more about trying to set an example, something about not engaging in casual sex."

"Casual sex?" he repeated with surprise, sitting up and swinging his legs around so he was facing her. "Is that what this feels like to you? Casual sex?"

Kate looked around to see if anyone was eavesdropping on their conversation, but they were the only two people on this part of the patio. "Actually, no, it doesn't feel like that. Maybe that's the problem. I thought I could treat this thing between us as something light, but I guess I'm not made that way, at least not anymore. Making love is too important, too"—she searched for a better word—"intimate to be casual."

"And you don't want to be intimate with me," T. R. said flatly, barely masking an undertone of hurt.

Kate looked at him. With his mouth set in a hard line and his nostrils flaring, she could tell that he was on the verge of covering up his hurt by lashing out at her. She hadn't seen him like this before, and it made her uncomfortable. "I'm sorry."

"Let me see if I get this," he said. "You don't want to make love with me because it's too casual. But wait, it's not that at all, it's that it's too important, make that *intimate*. Have I got it right?"

Kate could feel herself getting defensive again. "Something like that."

"Interesting logic you've got there."

"I said I'm sorry," she said, her own temper flaring.

"Sorry that your mind works like that?" he snapped out. "Sorry that I'm not real happy right now? Or sorry that we never got together?"

"All three, dammit. Okay?"

Their eyes locked, each of them on the edge of real, out-in-the-open anger. T. R. was the one who broke the tension by relaxing the muscles of his face into a grim smile.

"Okay," he said, nodding. "Okay."

Swinging his legs up, he resumed his prone position on his lounge, looking off toward the golf course that lay adjacent to the patio.

After a while he said quietly, "I learned a long time ago how destructive it can be to lose your temper, so I really try not to get into that. But it's real hard to keep my usual"—he laughed softly—"low-key, laid-back personality when I'm around you."

"Same here."

He angled his head so he was looking at her through lowered lids. "This isn't just about making love, Kate. What we have here is this . . . attraction. I don't know how deep it is, or how real it is, or how long it will last, but it's there."

He picked up her hand from the arm of her chair and kissed the knuckles lightly, then set it back down. "And when two grown-ups get this kind of thing going," he continued, covering her hand with his, "they usually express it by going to bed and finding out what it is that they have. So, I'm curious, Kate. What's the holdup? I mean, the real holdup?"

There was silence. He was waiting for her, she knew, but she had no answer. Her body yearned for him, but above the neck, in the storehouse of her mind where she made decisions and weighed the consequences, it didn't feel right.

"What do you want from me?" he asked.

"I wish I knew."

"Is it the musician thing?"

"Probably. Partly. I'm not sure."

He let go of her hand. "You're a fountain of self-knowledge, aren't you?" he said, his patience obviously at an end. "You take the prize. Man, I—No."

Sitting up again, he hunched over and rested his elbows on his knees, raking his hair with his long fingers several times. He took a deep breath then exhaled. "Forget I said that, okay? I'm acting a little nuts, but it's because I want you so much. From the moment I saw you on the beach. And it's difficult to walk around, frustrated all the time."

Kate looked down at her own tightly clenched

hands. "It's okay, you don't have to apologize. The way I'm acting, I don't blame you for being confused."

She closed her eyes for a moment, then opened them and looked up at the sky. The first faint pin-points of starlight were appearing. The beginning of the last night. But this sadness she was feeling had nothing to do with it being the end of her vacation. It was saying good-bye to T. R. that was making her feel on the edge of tears.

She turned to him, a wistful smile on her face. "Look, T. R. It's been a wonderful week. Being with you has been a lot of fun. Let's not turn it into a battle of wills, okay?"

His brows knitted into a scowl as he studied her face with intense concentration. She wanted to look away, but she forced herself to meet his piercing blue eyes for what seemed like a long time.

Finally, he expelled a sigh. "You're right. It has been a wonderful week. Just a little different than I'd hoped. And I won't spend our last night by coming on like some super stud and trying to talk you into bed. It's not my style. I think I'll take a walk instead." He gave a mirthless laugh. "I'm a little tense, I guess you could say."

Pushing himself up from the chair, he stood over her, his hands on his hips. As always, his rock-hard body and thoroughly masculine presence were overpowering.

"I'm going to say good-bye now, Kate. I don't want to, but I think I have to. You're quite a woman, you know, even if your thinking seems a little screwed-up." He leaned over and gave her a quick kiss on the cheek. "Have a safe trip back to L.A. Tell Dee good luck from me."

"So, I won't see you in the morning? Not even to say good-bye?"

"I don't think so. It wouldn't—"

He didn't finish his sentence, just shook his head

then gave her that cocky grin of his. With a little wave, he took off.

Kate leaned back in her chair, closing her eyes as a mood that was both confused and melancholy washed over her.

T. R. was gone.

She felt suddenly empty, as though a piece of her were missing.

She hadn't counted on feeling like this on her last night in Hawaii.

Five

T. R.'s fingers moved rapidly over the keys, betraying his frustration. He was only barely aware that he was in the hotel's piano bar, and that it was three o'clock in the morning. As far back as he could remember, whenever sleeplessness, anxiety, or sadness would come on him in the middle of the night, he'd noodle on the piano to soothe himself.

His nocturnal playing had been a joke with the other members of Pow!, the heavy-metal group he'd toured with for ten years. With three hundred one-nighters a year and all the dope and groupies they could handle, the other band members, once they fell asleep, were unconscious, gone to the world. But not T. R. Whatever action he'd seen earlier, he preferred to sleep alone, and when he couldn't sleep, he would play the piano for himself, often into the morning hours.

Tonight, after the scene with Kate, he'd wandered aimlessly around the resort complex, winding up here and thinking he might work on the film score he'd been hired to do. That was part of the reason he'd come to Hawaii, so he could compose in peace. Writing for films was a new challenge for him, one that he was insecure about, even with all the studying he'd been doing since the band broke up. He'd planned to work here without all the distractions—the phone, his broker, his agent, the fans.

Kate O'Brien had been a bigger distraction than all those put together. After a week, he'd gotten almost nothing done. Thank God she'd be on that plane in the morning and out of his life. Kate O'Brien screwed around with his head; she was a distraction he couldn't afford.

The silvery light of a full moon streamed in through an overhead skylight as he fingered an old standard. Finding some interesting chords, he played softly, his head bent over the keys. The sounds soothed his soul. Music was the answer to everything. It had always been there—and would outlast any woman in his life.

A quick movement across the room, something white, drew his attention away from his playing. He wasn't alone, dammit. He swiveled on the piano stool to glare at the intruder, but stopped in midturn.

Kate stood in the doorway, dressed in a long white garment, looking at him without smiling, her honey-colored hair hanging in soft waves to her shoulders. She was a vision. A ghost. An angel.

"Hi," he said softly, the hurt and anger of a moment ago evaporating magically at the sight of her.

"I couldn't sleep." Her words were spoken in a quiet, resigned tone.

"Yeah, me too. How long you been standing there?"

"Awhile. You look . . . beautiful when you play."

He felt embarrassed, self-conscious, at her use of the word. "I kind of go away when I get around a piano, I guess."

"I envy you."

He made a dismissive gesture. "Don't." Feeling his heart thudding loudly in his chest, he waited to see what she was going to do next.

She moved from the doorway, walking slowly toward him as though sleepwalking. The material of her shift was a thin cotton, nearly diaphanous in the moonlight. He inhaled sharply as she glided closer toward him, allowing him to discern the complete outline of her slender body with those high, full breasts and long legs. He ached for her. It was all he could do to stay still, but he did.

When she reached the piano, he sensed her nervousness as she stood at the edge of the keyboard, running her fingernail around the wood trim. She worried her lower lip with her teeth, and he could hear the gentle whoosh of air coming out of her nostrils, a little too fast, a little too loud. Like his own.

"T. R.," she said, studying her own hand.

"Hmm?"

"I . . . don't know how to say this—"

"Just say it," he prompted.

Nodding, she still couldn't seem to meet his eyes. "I would like to be with you tonight."

Raising an eyebrow questioningly, he leaned an elbow on the ridge near the music stand. "In what way?"

Finally, she looked at him, then lifted the corner of her mouth. "You're not going to make this any easier for me, are you?"

He grinned. "Uh-uh. I'm kind of enjoying this."

"Well, I'm kind of embarrassed."

Putting his hands around her waist, he rested his palms on the curved flare of her hips. The action pulled the see-through fabric tight over her breasts, so that the generous, creamy mounds with their pale brown nipples were more visible. The ache in his loins grew stronger. "Don't be. Tell me what you want."

She sighed. "I want to make love with you."

He could see her breasts rise and fall under the thin material, and desire, heavy and urgent, tightened his body. "So do I, Kate," he whispered. "So do I."

Pulling her toward him, he settled her in the V between his legs and put his arms around her, hugging her tightly to him for several moments. Then he eased her onto his lap and pulled her legs across his knees. Lifting her hair away from her neck, he buried his head there, breathing in the faint smell of orange blossoms and noting how she bowed back with pleasure the moment they touched.

"Oh, T. R.," she said, "I'm sorry I was so—"

"Forget it," he interjected. "You're here now . . . *querida.*"

Angling her face toward him, he covered her full, trembling mouth with his. The moment he tasted her sweetness, he wanted more. He raked his fingers through her hair, then bracketed her head with his hands so he could taste all of her—the luscious feel of her soft lips, the succulent flesh just inside her mouth. He sipped of her honey, savoring all her surfaces—the pearl-smooth ridges of teeth, the moist skin of her inner cheeks, the rough-yet-gentle texture of her tongue. She held on to his biceps as though clinging to life, her thumbs digging into his flesh as a little moan escaped from the back of her throat.

As T. R. continued his loving assault on her mouth, Kate granted him access, feeling the release of all the week's pent-up frustrations. She'd fought with herself about coming to him tonight, but now that she was here—her skin on fire, her breath speeding up with each new movement of his tongue and hands—she realized that there had never been a choice. That she and T. R. would be together, if only for this one night, seemed almost ordained, and any more struggle against its inevitability was both foolish and futile.

She tried to shift closer to him, wanting only to touch and be touched, every part of her, every section of skin connected, joined, intertwined. She eased one leg over his lap so that she was straddling him. Twisting her body into his, she rubbed her aching breasts against the taut muscles of his chest, her nipples hardening instantly into tight, throbbing buds.

As she squirmed restlessly, she could feel the solid bulge of his manhood beneath her. "Yes," she said, as he ran his hands over her with an impatience that matched her own, his sensitive, sensuous fingers lighting small fires across her shoulders, down her arms, over her hips, and under her buttocks, pulling her even closer, her legs even higher, so they were wrapped around his waist.

"*Querida.*" He tugged at the elastic around her neckline so he could lick the collarbone. "I feel like I've been waiting for you forever."

With her fingers wrapped in his thick black hair, she sighed as his mouth shifted lower. "*Querida,*" she repeated. "I like it when you say that. What does it mean?"

His velvety lips and knowing tongue nuzzled their way down into the valley between her breasts. "It's a kind of"—his voice was muffled in her sizzling skin, making her shiver all over—"affectionate term, you know, like 'honey' or 'darling.' "

"*Querida,*" she said again. "Darling." Closing her eyes, she arched back and offered her breasts to him. He nipped at first one, then the other, wrenching a cry of pleasure from her. After making tantalizing circles around the aureoles, he sucked at the nipples, first gently, then stronger, pulling the aching flesh into his mouth and bathing it with his tongue.

All thought was erased from her mind, leaving only sensation and fire. She cried out again as a sweet pain, a tightening between her legs, made her clamp her thighs around him tighter.

"Kate."

Her own heavy, labored breathing almost drowned out the sound of his voice. But his mouth—he had stopped adoring her breasts, and she couldn't stand it. Trying to pull his head closer, she said, "Don't stop. Please."

"Baby." He took her hands from behind his neck and clasped them between his own larger ones. "Making love on a piano works in the movies, but I think we need to go somewhere more private."

As his words filtered through the sensuous haze filling her head, she opened her eyes reluctantly. She looked at him, taking in the fine sheen of perspiration that covered his face, making his brandy-colored skin glisten silver in the moonlight. Lovingly, her gaze wandered over his high, chiseled cheekbones, the fine arch of his jet eyebrows, the flare of his wide nostrils as he took in the extra air demanded by his rapid respiration. Dear Lord, she thought, he was beautiful. "We can't go to my room. Dee's there."

"I know. The condo . . . ?"

"Too far," she said, shaking her head. Removing one hand from his grasp, she brushed a wayward lock of hair off his brow. The texture was like thick, heavy silk. "The beach," she said softly. "Please, T. R., I want to make love with you on the beach."

He chuckled. "That's another movie favorite."

"The movies have nothing to do with it. It's my last night in Hawaii, and I want it to be special." She felt suddenly almost shy and looked down, playing with a button on his shirt collar. "Will you make it special for me?" she asked in a small voice.

His sharp intake of air signaled his eagerness to make it very special. "You got it." Placing her hands behind his neck, and tucking her legs more securely around his waist, he rose from the piano bench with a fluid movement that belied the weight he was holding in his arms.

"You don't have to carry me," she murmured against his neck.

"You're barefoot."

"Am I? I didn't realize. I left my room in a kind of dream state."

"And I'm so glad you did."

She sighed into him, feeling his warm breath on her hair and the throbbing of his pulse point against her mouth as he walked them out across the deserted patio and onto the beach. With only the glow of the full moon lighting their way, T. R. rounded a curve at the shoreline, taking them to a small grove of palm trees tucked away near the cabanas. Setting her down, he said, "Wait here."

Kate stood where he'd told her to, shivering in her thin gown, but not with cold. Desire, still simmering just beneath the surface, darted along all her nerve endings, sending small jolts of electricity through her. Hugging herself, she looked around. Under the black night sky, with its silvery globe of a moon, she felt as if there were no one else in the world except her and the man who would soon be her lover. Her heartbeat accelerated till she could hear it pounding in her ears. But for the soft swishing of waves, all else was silent.

T. R. returned with a thick pad from one of the oversize lounge chairs that lay in rows along the shoreline. Placing it on a smooth, flat section of sand under a towering palm, he turned to Kate and smiled. "Will this do?" When she nodded, he held out his arms to her. "Come here, then," he ordered softly.

She moved into the cradle of his embrace and, with one fluid motion, he lowered them both onto the mat, pulling her close against him. "Kate O'Brien," he murmured into her hair.

"Why do you like to say my whole name?"

"I don't know," he said, his warm tongue sending more shivers down the side of her neck as he licked around her ear. "It's musical, I guess. Soft. Irish. Delicious, like your skin."

He loosened his hold on her slightly, and Kate lay on her back, her arms above her head. Then he brought his body over hers so that he was half on top of her, his knee between her thighs. She inhaled sharply as he looked at her, his eyes serious and searching. With his thumb tracing all the contours of her face, he said, "I'm so glad you changed your mind."

Her eyes closed automatically at his sensuous exploration. "Somehow I don't think my mind had anything to do with it."

He shifted his body slightly and laced his fingers in hers. With slow, sensual caresses, velvet lips kissed and licked around her brows, her eyelids, along the curve of her cheek. Finally, she felt the moist tip of his tongue as he ran it over her quivering lips.

She sighed. "T. R. You—Oh."

"I what, *querida?*"

"You make me feel like the most desirable woman in the world."

"But you are, Kate O'Brien," he said huskily. "You are."

He kissed her, his mouth hot and tasting of passion, and she met his kiss with open fervor as they joined tongues and teeth, tasting each other, biting gently, then harder. The fever took hold of them, burning hotter and hotter, begging for release.

T. R. fought his body's need for instant gratification. He'd been aching for her all week, and now, with a seeming mind of its own, his body no longer wanted to wait for satisfaction. Nevertheless, he concentrated on prolonging their lovemaking as he eased the shift off her shoulder, sending a trail of kisses along each inch of uncovered flesh. When her breasts were bared, he marveled at their round, pale beauty, and cupped them, loving the way the full mounds filled his palms, hardening and thrusting out to seek his touch.

He massaged them both with eager hands, molding and pushing them toward each other. Kate let out a thin cry when his hot mouth closed over both nipples, sucking them strongly. He felt the shudder that pulsed all through her, duplicating the one that was taking over his own fevered body. When her hips began to move in that ancient, automatic rotation that signaled readiness, he stripped the rest of the garment off her, until she was completely unclothed.

At the sight of her white, flawless skin—the moonlight cast shadows under her chin, the crescents of her womanly breasts, the indentation at the belly button, the pale triangle of curls between her legs—T. R. shook his head in wonder. "I can't believe how beautiful your body is," he said, skimming his hands all over her, from the pulse at her neck to her ankles.

"T. R." Kate gazed at him, her clear blue eyes turning pale gray in the moonlight. "I want to see you. Please."

She started to undo his buttons, but her hands were shaking so hard, he wound up doing it himself. When he'd discarded the shirt, she ran her hands along his broad shoulders, her nails digging into the layers of muscle that corded his arms.

"You're so . . . firm," she said. "So strong."

"It's genetic. All the men in my family are built like this."

"And the women in your family are very glad."

He chuckled, then drew in a breath as she rubbed her palms back and forth over his chest, tracing the flesh there. "Your skin," she said on a sigh, "it's like nothing I've ever felt before. Smooth, like living glass."

Kate couldn't seem to stop touching him, enjoying his gasp of pleasure when her fingertips grazed his nipple. Sliding her palms up and down his naked back, she felt the hard ripple of muscle under his warm skin. And all the while her body grew heavier and more liquid, as a deep inner throbbing made her move restlessly against him.

T. R. unzipped the loose cotton pants he'd worn earlier, giving silent thanks for the protection he'd been carrying all week that was still there in his wallet. Good thing, too, he thought, because with Kate touching him like this, moving her hips provocatively, and with the fire in his hardened loins pulsing between his legs, he knew that nothing would stop him now.

He discarded the rest of his clothes quickly, and lay back on the mat, pulling Kate to him.

"Wait," she said. "I'm not finished exploring you yet."

He was vaguely aware of the sound of slapping waves, the stars overhead and warm, sultry breezes that engulfed both of them like a loving cloak. The touch of her was almost more than he could bear; her fingertips brushed all over him, down over the muscled ridge of his stomach and across his hips and thighs. As his rapidly beating heart sped up even more, he could hear her ragged breaths mingle with his in the night air. "Baby," he groaned, "I don't know how much longer I can take this."

"A little longer. Please." She traced the muscle along his calf. "I've wanted to touch you like this all week."

"Well, what kept you from doing it?"

"I can't think of a reason right now."

Kate brought her hand up over his sturdy thighs. "You're the one with a beautiful body." Gently, she cupped his surging manhood. "Especially this," she whispered.

Slowly, enticingly, she encircled him with her hand and moved deliberately down the length of him. "Easy, easy," he said hoarsely, not wanting her to stop but knowing he was perilously close to having it end too quickly. "Wait."

He twisted his body away from her and, reaching into the pocket of his pants, retrieved the condom. "I need to put this on."

In spite of the haze of sensuality she was in, Kate was dimly aware of gratitude toward T. R. for remembering to take care of this; she'd been thrown so off center by her attraction to him, she'd neglected everything else. "Let me," she said.

She took the foil-wrapped package and opened it. Placing the condom on the tip of his shaft, she rolled it down over him, loving the feel of his hard heat between her fingers, and both thrilled and a bit frightened at the thought of this thick, powerful organ inside her.

"It feels so much better when you do it than when I do," T. R. rasped.

She laughed softly. "I wonder why."

"Now me." He turned her onto her back and, as he kissed her mouth with almost desperate fervor, he reached down and pushed her legs apart. Stroking her inner thighs, he wrung a wordless cry of need from her as his fingers touched the moist, throbbing flesh between her legs. Kate gasped against his mouth and arched up into his hand.

Waves of pleasure assaulted her, each one stronger than the one before, as he found the small, hot nub buried in the curls there and rubbed and stroked her to the point of insanity.

"Wet, so wet," he said, his voice hoarse with urgency. Inserting his long finger into the warm, moist cave of her femininity, he moaned. "Kate, I—"

"*Now*, T. R.," she said, spreading her legs farther apart for him. She couldn't stop the rotating movement of her hips. She ached, she wanted him so. "Please, now."

"Yes." He moved over her and, bringing her hands to either side of her head and holding them flat against the pad, he surged into her with one powerful thrust, kissing her at the same time and taking her cry of wonder into his mouth.

Kate knew no sense of time or location—the stars, the sea, the planet, all gone. There was only now, only the feel of T. R.'s strong, masculine body as it surged into her repeatedly, invading her, forcing her muscles to make room for him, filling her and blocking out everything but the spiraling physical need spreading all through her.

Again and again, he thrust into her, and again and again she moaned his name, moving with him, her skin so hot, it felt like wildfire. Waves of physical ecstasy began to crash upon her. With a strangled cry—"T. R.!"—she went over the top into total oblivion.

T. R., through the roaring in his ears, heard her call out his name and felt her muscles clench his manhood in quivering spasms. With one final thrust into her, he let it go, releasing his seed, his tension, his very soul.

He collapsed on her, letting the small aftershocks, the tiny little convulsions that pulsated through both their bodies, wear themselves out so that he and Kate could settle down once again. Finally, a sense of calm returned.

"Kate," he murmured in her ear as he withdrew from her and onto his side, not wanting to break the bond between them yet, but afraid his weight was too much for her. Cradling her in the curve of his arm, he kissed her forehead. *"Querida."*

"Mmm" was all she said.

T. R. woke with a start and sat up, causing the shirt that was draped loosely over him to fall around his waist. Looking around him, disoriented, he realized that he was on the beach; it was still dark outside, and he was sitting on the pad that he and Kate had used as their bed.

But where was Kate? Back at her room, of course, he answered himself as his head cleared. They had fallen asleep in each other's arms, he remembered that, so she must have awakened first, covered him up as best she could, and left.

Lying back down, he gazed up at the starry night. The moon had traveled across the sky, so it was probably about a half hour before dawn. He stretched his arms above his head, still tired but wonderfully content. That was because of Kate, of course. He smiled at the thought of her, at the thought of the two of them, together.

Kate O'Brien.

Finally.

Funny how he was feeling about it. He'd been so determined, that first day on the beach, to get the high school cheerleader into his bed. He'd wanted her—man, how he'd wanted her—nineteen years' worth. And earlier tonight, she'd been his.

And yet there was no sense of triumph, no feeling of a job well done. Making love with Kate had meant something completely different, something that had nothing to do with fulfilling an old fantasy. It had been . . . heartfelt. Special.

Thinking about Kate now, T. R. wanted her again; it was as though his body, tasting her sweetness once, required more. A lot more.

But not only in bed.

This whole thing was strangely disturbing, as though a door had opened, just slightly, into a new world. He wasn't quite sure if he wanted to go through it to the other side.

Why, he wondered, had he felt so *complete* with her, so right? Sure, his body had reacted with relief, gratitude even, but there were tuggings on other parts of him—his mind, his heart. This had been more than coupling, it had been a mingling of souls.

"A mingling of souls?" he said aloud. Man, he thought, shaking his head, what was with him, using phrases like that? It didn't sound like him, not in the least.

Used to be, he didn't even believe in that stuff. What the hell was happening here?

Pulling on his clothes, T. R. made his way to the condo, yawning. He would set his alarm for a couple of hours from now and meet her for breakfast. They'd make plans to meet in L.A.

Whatever was going down here, one night with Kate O'Brien wasn't going to be enough. That was for sure.

"Fool."

Shaking her head with disgust, Kate stared at her bleary-eyed image in the bathroom mirror. Even with her body free of tension, drugged with satisfaction, she was already regretting her wild joining with T. R. under the stars. She'd been right, she couldn't treat her feelings for him casually.

"Fool," she said again. Out on the beach, with a full silvery moon above, it had been magic. In all her life, she had never been so thoroughly aroused, had never been made love to like that. She was under no illusion that she could have avoided it—she'd *had* to go to him earlier.

Still, by searching him out in the middle of the night, by opening up not just her body but her heart to him, she was playing with fire and knew it. She didn't and never would regret the act itself, at least. But she truly, deeply regretted feeling the way she did about him.

She was half in love with him already, she admitted to herself, and that was to court disaster. Any further contact with T. R. would be self-destructive; she'd given up that kind of behavior years ago. Musicians were unreliable, the original heartbreakers. After Alan took off and John let her down, she'd vowed that she'd never again let a music man toss her emotions around. Kate intended to keep that vow.

After splashing cold water on her face, she went into the bedroom and shook her sleeping daughter. "Dee, wake up."

"Hmm?"

Kate pulled the covers off. "Come on, honey, we've got to get going."

Dee sat up in bed, her coppery hair sticking up in the air like porcupine spikes. "What time is it?"

"Six."

Dee rubbed the heels of her hands across her eyes. "But the plane doesn't leave for hours."

"We're going to the airport early," Kate said, moving toward the dresser and throwing the contents of the drawers into a large suitcase. "Get packed. We'll eat there."

"But, Mom—" Dee began.

"Don't 'But, Mom' me," she snapped, then caught herself and added in a more conciliatory tone, "I'm sorry, honey, but I forgot to get gifts for Grandma and Aunt Tress, and for the girls in the shop. I promised everyone fresh pineapples—they have all that at the airport."

Her daughter looked at her as if she were about to protest once again, but something on Kate's face discouraged her. "Bummer," Dee muttered, then hopped out of bed with her usual early morning animation and took herself off to the bathroom.

Suddenly dejected, Kate sat on the edge of the bed, grateful not to have to answer any more questions. Because she wasn't sure she could.

All she knew was that last night she'd been sure she'd never want to leave Hawaii, and this morning she needed to get as far away from the island as she could.

Six

" . . . so much garlic in the sauce, I thought they were expecting a vampire at the table."

"It was the most darling little dress I'd ever seen, and it was only five hundred."

"It's been over a year now, but I still keep seeing him on the street, walking that little dachshund of his . . ."

" . . . one of those rehab programs, you know, like you hear about on *Oprah*."

The soft sibilance of female gossip and laughter, with oldies rock music playing in the background, were so familiar that Kate hardly noticed them anymore. At Annabella, while their nails were being repaired, buffed, filed, wrapped, and painted, clients told their manicurists the most intimate details about their lives. Here they had a sympathetic, mostly trustworthy ear for an hour a week; when they left, they knew that not only were their hands beautiful, but their secrets were safe.

Right now, Kate was tending to her 8:00 A.M. Thursday appointment, an elderly, fussy woman who shared with Kate every detail of the second-floor addition she and her husband were building in their home. Kate nodded and said the appropriate "mm-hm"s and "oh?"s as the woman discussed wallpapers and wall sconces, but Kate was on automatic pilot, not paying attention at all.

Instead, she was on a beach in Hawaii under a full moon. A thickly muscled man with long black hair and vivid blue eyes was making the most beautiful love to her. Waves and sand and palm trees filled her head. In the week since she'd been back at work, she had revisited this scene several times in her dreams, awake and asleep. She wondered when her mind would cease to form this picture, and when the sense of sadness, of feeling alone—as if a part of her were missing—would stop invading her.

"So, what do you think? Cantaloupe or Apricot Blush?"

"What?" Kate said. "Oh, excuse me, Mrs. Patterson. What did you say?"

"Which color nail polish shall I have today?" her client asked with a slight querulousness.

"Definitely the apricot." Kate chastised herself for drifting off like that. Mrs. Patterson always tipped well at Christmas. Kate needed to remember to pay attention and stop this ridiculous habit she'd developed of slipping away into her imagination.

"Are you sure?"

Kate beamed a smile on the woman. "Absolutely. It's wonderful with your skin tone."

After her client left to choose bathroom tile, Kate went into the small kitchen that was off the salon's large, airy main room. There were usually some homemade cookies there, courtesy of Bella. Sure enough, it was lemon bars today, and Kate munched on one. She hadn't had breakfast that morning and was hungry.

After eating two of the crisp confections, she peeked into the room, but her nine o'clock still hadn't climbed the stairs from the gift shop below. If the cookies were very good, they were also very sweet, so Kate put a cup under the cooler faucet for some water, but before she could taste it, it slipped from her hand and all over the linoleum.

"Good, Kate. Really graceful," she muttered to herself as she mopped up the floor.

"You know you're in trouble when you start talking to yourself. How's it going?"

Mop in hand, Kate looked up. Bella stood in the doorway, her warm brown eyes filled with gentle concern. Kate shook her head. "I don't know. I seem to be remarkably clumsy lately."

"Since you came back from vacation, actually." Bella grabbed a handful of paper towels and gave her a hand with the cleanup effort. "What is it? That man you met?"

"Perish the thought."

Bella put the towels in the trash container, then leaned against the counter, her tall, rounded body and high cheekbones giving her the air of a large-size fashion model at rest. "Come on, Kate. This is me, Bella. Remember? Talk to me."

Kate shrugged. "Maybe I need another week of vacation."

"Maybe you don't want to talk about that man."

"I'm sorry I told you about him."

Bella smiled. "You had no choice. I dragged it out of you."

"Well, how about we erase that conversation? I'm fine, okay?" Kate insisted emphatically, even though it was far from the truth.

"Maybe if you say it one more time you'll believe it."

"Ooh!" Kate threw up her hands and went back into the salon to wait for her next appointment.

As she picked up a magazine, the phone rang. After the third ring, she looked around, hoping someone else would take it. Bella was still in the kitchen. Diane was busy with a client. So were Donna, Ernestine, and Lois. Kate closed the magazine and picked up the phone.

"Annabella. May I help you?" She reached for the large black appointment book. It seemed the caller's daughter had come into town unexpectedly, and could she change her pedicure with Lois from tomorrow morning to the following morning? Of course, that would mean her manicure with Donna would have to be shifted, too, but if Donna wasn't available, might Kate have some free time on her schedule? Or one of the others?

She was so busy writing and erasing in the book that she failed to notice when the silence first descended on the usually noisy room. The music was still on, but all conversation had ceased. How strange, Kate thought. She looked up, wondering what could possibly have happened.

And then she knew.

A man stood at the top of the stairs. That in itself was highly unusual—only rarely did the occasional husband or male client ever enter this feminine enclave. And this newcomer was not only male, but one of those males who stopped traffic.

It was T. R.

He was dressed all in white—a white T-shirt under a white linen suit. The contrast against his golden bronze skin, with his black hair falling loosely around his shoulders, an errant lock dipping low across his forehead, was enough to start Kate's heart beating erratically. Lord, he was gorgeous! Standing there on the landing at the top of the stairs, his eyes roaming around the room restlessly, he looked for all the world like a cross between an outlaw and a movie star. No wonder all the chatter in the shop had ceased; everyone's attention was riveted on this rooster in the henhouse.

T. R.'s gaze came to rest on Kate. He gave her one of his slow, lazy smiles, and she felt herself blush. She never blushed, she thought. What was the matter with her? So he was here. Big deal.

But the next moment, her nonchalant attitude underwent a 180-degree turnaround. He's here, she thought with mounting excitement. He had come after her. One night wasn't enough for him, either.

However, she told herself with another rapid mood shift, there was the downside: He'd come after her. Hadn't he gotten the message? By running off like that after they'd made love, hadn't she made it perfectly clear that she wanted nothing more to do with him? She wanted him to stay away from her.

Or did she?

He kept staring at her, as if he expected her to do something. While she herself was still paralyzed, the other women were coming back to life, looking from him to her and back again to him. By degrees, the sound returned to the shop, little whispers, little gossipy murmurs.

Kate felt the flush on her face getting rosier by the second and was suddenly aware of an annoyed voice on the telephone. "Miss? Are you listening to me?"

"I'm so sorry," she said into the receiver. "We had a . . . little disturbance here." An earthquake. "I think I've got this all worked out now. See you Saturday morning at ten." She hung up the phone and put the appointment book back in its place. Maybe when she looked back up at the stairway landing, he would be gone.

No such luck. He was still there, but now a woman worked her way around him, saying, "Excuse me." It was Carla Stellini, Kate's next appointment, who—unaware that there was a minidrama in the making—sat herself down in the chair, saying, "Hi. Sorry I'm late."

Kate gave T. R. a pleading look, silently begging him not to embarrass her. After a few moments he smiled enigmatically, bowed slightly, and walked back down the stairs. There was a collective exhalation from the onlookers, followed by a few soft whistles and laughter.

Kate realized she hadn't said anything yet to Carla, who was looking at her with curiosity. "Who was that?" her client asked.

"Oh, just a man I met in Hawaii."

Carla smiled knowingly. "I'll bet that's not the end of the story."

"Carla, don't." Kate got up abruptly, taking a small glass dish over to the sink and filling it with warm, soapy water. Carla, a successful entertainment lawyer, was one of Kate's favorite clients, one Kate considered a friend. But Kate didn't want to answer any questions about T. R.

Besides, she had her own questions. Where had he gone just now? she wondered. And what did he mean, popping up like that and then taking off? What was he up to?

Would she ever see him again?

While Carla soaked her fingers in the water, Kate got her a cup of coffee from the kitchen, trying to tamp down all thoughts of T. R. and having no success at all. As she was setting the steaming cup down on the table, it teetered precariously on the edge, and only quick intervention from Carla prevented it from spilling all over her lap, possibly causing serious burns.

Kate covered her mouth with her hand. "Carla, I'm so sorry."

"No problem," her friend said easily. "Nothing happened. Now sit down and talk to me."

Kate knew that she continued to be an object of speculation by the other women in the room and that her face was still registering flushed discomfort. On top of which, her clumsiness had nearly caused a painful accident. T. R. had an incredible, unsettling effect on her—it simply wasn't fair. "Why did he have to come here, dammit?" she muttered as she sat down and tore off a piece of cotton from the large glass canister on the table.

"What's his name?" Carla asked while Kate removed the old polish from her left hand.

"Who?" Kate said distractedly.

"The hunk in white."

"T. R. something." Suddenly, Kate realized she didn't even remember his last name.

"He looks familiar."

"Dee said the same thing. He's a musician."

"Studio? Rock? With a band?" In her profession, Carla knew a lot of people in the music industry.

"Rock, I'm pretty sure, and he used to be with a band, I think he said. Now he just—I don't know—travels and plays." She paused, puzzled. "Actually, I don't really know what he does."

"Didn't get around to finding out, huh?"

"Carla—" Kate warned.

"Too busy with other activities, I guess." Carla grinned like the proverbial Cheshire cat.

It was difficult not to smile back, but Kate fixed her client with what she hoped was a stern glare. "Ms. Stellini, if you value your Thursday morning appointment time, you'll stop this line of questioning right now."

"Not in the mood for 'sharing' today?" Carla asked sweetly.

"You got it."

"Okay, I'll be good. I could never give up my Thursday mornings."

T. R. walked down the stairs deep in thought. It had been good to see Kate again; at the sight of her, he'd felt a surge of warmth in his chest. She'd seemed pretty pleased to see him, too, then angry, then embarrassed. She'd gone through a hell of a lot of emotions.

Well, this last week his emotions had run the gamut too. After she snuck away from him in

Hawaii, checking out of her room early, he was pissed off and decided to forget her. Who needed a woman who kept fighting her attraction to him as if it might kill her? Trying to put her out of his mind, he had worked on his film score and looked around for another woman who might take his fancy. But in spite of the bikini fashion show on the beach, and the available ladies giving him the eye in the lounge, he could think only of Kate, of wanting Kate, of aching for Kate.

So here he was in L.A., over a week before he was due here for the session, and way behind on the score. This whole thing was completely out of character for him. Never, in all his life, had he pursued a woman with so much dogged determination, to the detriment of his music. But there was no way she was getting away from him this time. They were going to meet, at least once, and hash this thing out.

"Did you find Kate all right?" The lilting English accent came from the petite young woman behind the counter. T. R. looked around, noticing the shop and its contents for the first time. He'd been so intent on seeing Kate when he first came in, he'd scarcely been aware of his surroundings. He was in a gift shop, he now saw, the kind that had small items with large price tags.

"Yes, thanks," he said. "What's that smell?"

"Potpourri. Lemon verbena today."

"I like it. It isn't too, you know, perfumy."

The young woman pointed to a highly polished table on which was displayed a collection of lace pillows. "The woman who makes them for me gathers herbs from her garden and uses bits of antique wedding gowns for the pillow covers. My customers like to put them in their lingerie drawers."

He wanted to buy one for Kate. Looking around the shop, he wanted to buy a lot of things for Kate. He also wanted to wring Kate's neck.

"I'm Hollis," said the young woman, coming around the counter and offering him her hand. "This is my shop, Annabella Deux."

As he returned the handshake, he noticed how small she was and delicate looking. Somehow he doubted that she was as fragile as she appeared. "T. R. Beltran," he said. "If you're Hollis, you sent Kate flowers in Hawaii." At her look of surprise, he smiled. "I was there when she received them."

"Were you?" Hollis studied him more carefully. "Kate's my friend."

He chuckled. "I'd like Kate to be my friend too. May I use your phone? I'll be glad to pay for the call."

"Is it local?"

"About as local as you can get. Upstairs. I'll need the number."

At first, Hollis looked puzzled. Then she laughed and pointed to the small desk in the corner of the shop. "The number's next to the phone. And—T. R. is it?"

He nodded.

"I wish you luck."

"Kate!" Bella called from across the room. "Phone."

Tucking the receiver between her ear and shoulder so her hands were free to work on Carla's cuticles, Kate said, "Yes?"

"Hi."

T. R. didn't have to say any more than that for her blood to begin to percolate. "Hello," she replied, her voice cracking as she spoke.

"Shall I do the drill about how are you?" he asked.

"I don't think so. Where are you calling from?"

"Downstairs. Annabella Deux, right?"

"Mm-hm." She made herself concentrate on Carla's manicure.

"Nice. Very lacy kind of place. It made me think of you." There was silence for a moment, then she heard him expel a breath. "Kate O'Brien, I don't know what I'm going to do with you."

"Pardon?"

"You don't make it easy, do you? Listen, let's get together—dinner, a cup of coffee, you call it."

"I don't think—"

He interrupted. "You owe me."

"I what?"

"I said you owe me. An explanation, at least. Why did you split like that? Was that last night we were together such a bad experience that you had to run away?"

She felt the color coming to her face again. Carla was making no attempt to look away, so Kate lowered her voice and turned her head. "You know it wasn't."

"Then why?"

"Please, don't—"

"Please don't what?"

She swallowed. "You're angry."

He sighed again into the phone. "No, it's okay. I think I'm . . . hurt, actually."

"I'm sorry."

"Don't sweat it, I'm a big boy. Where do you want to meet?"

"I'm at work."

"I know," he said. "That's why I'm asking you to meet me afterward. Tonight, if possible. Are you available?"

She felt paralyzed, unable to answer him.

"How about the Café Figaro on Melrose?" he persisted. "Seven o'clock. It's loud and public, so you don't have to be afraid."

"I'm not afraid."

"Maybe you'd prefer someplace quieter?" His voice took on that soft, sensual tone that she remembered from their night on the beach. "Someplace more private."

"No, no, Figaro will be fine. Make it seven-thirty."

"Good. And, Kate?"

"Yes?"

"Show up, all right?"

"I will. But just for a cup of coffee."

"Coffee's a start."

She was late. Her final manicure had had weak, difficult nails, and the appointment had gone over-time. Then traffic from the westside had been even worse than usual, and parking in this section of West Hollywood, where there were so many trendy clubs and restaurants, was a joke. After finding a space three blocks away and hurrying to get to the restaurant, when she finally entered the large, funky throwback to the sixties that was the Figaro, Kate wasn't in the best of moods. Not only was she tired and out of breath, but her anxiety level was pretty high; she was sorry she'd agreed to come at all.

Her eyes searched the crowded room, with its dark wooden beams and hanging plants, and came to rest immediately on T.R.—his white clothing made him stand out from everyone else. He was seated at a round wooden table in the far corner, near a window. His chair was tipped back, and he was leaning against the wall, his hands clasped behind his head. From what she could tell, the expression on his face was neutral. As she got closer to him, his lips curved in a slight smile, but she saw a faint pulse of tension in his jawline, as though he was clenching and unclenching his teeth.

With that pantherlike grace of his, he pushed himself away from the wall and stood as she approached. Her heart slammed against her chest at the sight of him, in his T-shirt that lovingly molded his broad upper body, and the jacket and pants that hung on his frame as if he had been the inspiration for their design. His presence was over-powering; he was still the most potently masculine man she'd ever met.

She'd agreed to meet him tonight because he was right—she did owe him an explanation of why she'd run away from him. She also intended to explain why there was no room for someone like him in her life. But now, gazing at him and feeling the familiar heat rising in her, Kate wondered how she'd ever thought she would come out of this unscathed.

"Lookin' good, Kate O'Brien," T. R. said, finally relaxing inside now that she was here. He'd half expected her to stand him up.

"Really?" She looked confused, almost disoriented.

"I like that outfit." He indicated the extra-long turquoise T-shirt that she wore over flower-patterned leggings. Her hair was in a high ponytail. "You look cute."

She made a face. "This is how I dress for work—there wasn't enough time to go home and change."

"You never have to dress up for me, didn't you know that? Grab a seat."

He moved behind a curve-backed chair and brought it out from the table for her. She looked at him as though taken aback by his courtliness, then she sat down.

He signaled the waiter. "What'll you have?" T. R. asked, making sure she was settled before he went back to his seat. "Wine? Beer? A Café Figaro?"

"Which is . . . ?"

"Chocolate, steamed milk, espresso, and whipped cream," recited the bespectacled young man who came up to the table.

"Have one," T. R. said.

She shook her head. "Just coffee, I think. It's been a long day."

"One coffee," T. R. told the waiter, "and I'll have whatever designer water you've got, with a twist."

"Will you be ordering dinner?"

T. R. looked at Kate. "Will we?"

"I'm not sure."

"We'll let you know," he said.

After the young man had gone, Kate said, "You're not having a drink?"

"I try to stay away from the hard stuff. It gets to be a pretty bad habit. But hell"—he grinned—"you already know how much all us musicians love the sauce, don't you?"

She arched one eyebrow. "You're never going to forgive me for that night, are you?"

"You mean, the night when you told me everything I've ever wanted to know about myself and every other musician in the world? I forgave you long ago. Now tell me," he said, shifting to small talk, "why has it been a long day?"

"On Thursdays, I go from eight in the morning to seven at night."

"No kidding."

"The same on Fridays and Saturdays. Those are the three busiest days in the nail business."

He nodded. "In the music business too. We're both geared to making sure people have fun on the weekends."

"And holidays."

He nodded. "And holidays. For a lot of years I spent every New Year's Eve up on a bandstand, playing 'Auld Lang Syne,' watching everyone else make complete fools of themselves and wishing like hell I could be one of them."

"And now? Do you still work on New Year's Eve?"

"No, I . . . don't have to do that anymore."

This was the perfect moment to tell her what he'd neglected to tell her before. About the years with Pow! The enormous amounts of adulation and money. The drug-overdose death of his best friend, the band's guitarist. The years since, getting his head on straight, making investments, learning how to read and write music properly for the first time in his life. The moment had come to tell Kate that he was no longer the irresponsible and flighty kid he used to be, that he was now a grown-up. If she knew the truth, she'd probably be less frightened of getting involved with him.

But something held him back, that same old feeling about wanting her to want to be with him without knowing how successful and wealthy and responsible he was. He didn't trust easily—children of alcoholics never did—and T. R. wanted to trust Kate. He would tell her some of it, but not all. Maybe he was being dishonest, or at least avoiding the truth, but he couldn't do it. Not yet.

The waiter brought their drinks and, for a few moments, they sat without talking. T. R. sensed Kate starting to unwind, maybe not even regretting anymore that she'd shown up. When he'd first seen her, she'd looked ready to bolt. "How's Dee?" he asked.

Kate took a sip of coffee. "Complaining that school starts in two weeks. In love with some new teen heartthrob on television. Losing her hearing from that damned ghetto-blaster. Skinny. Sweet. About like always."

"She's a great kid. She seems to have her head on straight."

"Really?" She looked pleased. "I can't tell, I'm too close."

"I've met a lot of teenagers. She's one of the good ones. I like her a lot."

Kate looked down, moving the saltshaker back and forth. "She likes you too."

He wanted to say, Do *you* like me? but thought he'd better not. "I asked you once how you wound up being a manicurist, and you told me it was a long story."

"It's still a long story."

He sat back in his chair and propped an ankle on his knee. "I have all the time in the world. My next job isn't for a week."

"Is that a problem? I mean, don't you need to keep working?"

"Sure. But when you free-lance, there are always these in-between times. I kick back while they're here, because when I do work, it's day and night."

"I see." She took another sip of her coffee.

"So, tell me."

She put down her cup and leaned her elbows on the table. "I became a manicurist because I needed to earn a decent living, and beauty school offered the best bet. I had just graduated high school and, like most eighteen-year-olds, had absolutely no skills at all."

With a wry smile she added, "What I did have was a daughter . . . and no husband. Dee is what they used to call a love child. But I suppose you've figured that out already."

Seven

T. R. nodded calmly and said, "I thought it was something like that. Alan, right? The trombone player."

"How did you know?"

"Elementary arithmetic. Dee's sixteen. You're thirty-three. Had to be in your senior year."

"But you weren't at Culver High when I got pregnant."

"No, but I sat in on marching-band rehearsals for those few months I was there, and old Alan, well, he used to talk about you with a hell of a lot of enthusiasm." Before she could say anything, T. R. held up his hands. "Hey, don't get me wrong—no juicy little bed details, none of that stuff."

"Thank God for small favors," Kate muttered. "Besides, there were no details to talk of, not then. The nuns had made quite an impression on me when I was younger. Alan and I went together for over a year before I let him touch me below the waist." She laughed, thinking about what she'd just said. "Remember? Above the waist, below the waist, all the way, French-kissing—all the expressions we used. We were so young."

"Yeah."

Talking to T. R. like this, relaxed and easy, Kate realized she was actually enjoying herself. She'd expected to be a wreck by now, but that first sense of discomfort, of total disorientation, was gone. In fact, she was in the mood for a nice long visit, not to mention a refresher on her coffee. She felt alive for the first time in a week. It was so good to see him!

She'd wondered, in Hawaii, why the two of them never just sat down and talked. True, they were always going somewhere to see a sight, and there were usually other people around. Then, when they were alone, there was that sexual tension that made conversation a strain. But mostly, Kate had to admit, it was because she had steered the talk away from personal histories and the trading of life experiences. Deep down, she'd been defending herself, reasoning, however foolishly, that the less she knew of T. R. and the less he knew of her, the easier it would be to say good-bye.

As she looked around the room for a waiter with a carafe of fresh coffee, T. R. moved his chair so he was sitting adjacent to instead of across from her. "The decibel level in this place is incredible," he explained. "Now, we don't have to shout to be heard."

She smiled, enjoying having him closer to her, enjoying it very much. "Good thinking. Tell me, what did Alan say about me?"

"You really want to know?"

"It's a long time ago. I think I can handle it."

She caught the eye of a passing waiter, and he came over and poured her some more of the delicious, cinnamon-flavored brew.

"Just guy stuff," T. R. said when they were alone again. "We all agreed that he had the best babe, the hottest-looking chick. He was admired and envied for going with Kate O'Brien, the cheerleader with the body that wouldn't quit. That kind of thing." He left out some of the other choice phrases they'd all used; there was no need to let her know the extent of the cruel shallowness of teenage boys.

"Was I really thought of as such a . . . sex object? I had no idea. Probably good that I didn't. On the other hand, I do remember something they used to whisper behind my back—Katy did or Katy didn't."

"That too," he said. "It was a favorite expression. We all wondered."

"After I started showing, in my senior year, they didn't bother with the 'Katy didn't' part."

They both stopped smiling at the same time. "Was it rough?" he asked quietly.

"Very. In more ways than one. Alan wanted me to get rid of the baby, but I couldn't do it. So, he took off about a month before graduation, went on a USO tour of the Orient with a band, and that was the end of that."

T. R. shook his head. "The son of a bitch."

Kate went on, telling her story simply, without a trace of self-pity. "I was determined to finish high school, and I did. But there were always cracks from the other kids about putting out and getting knocked up, and lectures from my parents about abstinence."

"You were pretty strong to get through all that."

"I didn't think of myself as strong. I cried every night."

"Did you miss Alan?"

She nodded. "At first. I felt . . . abandoned. We'd been together for two years, and he was the only guy I'd ever dated. My first love."

T. R. fought down a surprising surge of jealousy, along with the urge to wring Alan's neck. Chill out, he told himself. Being with Kate made all kinds of emotions come up, emotions he hadn't let himself feel for years, if ever. It was too much, too deep. He wasn't sure if he liked these sensations at all.

"Then," she went on, "I finally started getting angry, really pissed off. If he'd come back into town that year, I might have done something really ugly to him. My father would have, for sure."

"How did your folks take it?"

"As best they could. They didn't go to church for a while because they got all those sideways, disapproving looks. But I have to give them credit—they left it up to me as to what I wanted to do. I had never thought about having a child, and up until a month before she was born, I was still considering putting her up for adoption. But I couldn't." Her expression softened as she looked inward with a gentle smile. "The moment I saw that wrinkled little face next to me on the bed, she was mine."

"Mother love," he said softly, as another strong surge of feeling swept over him.

"It's the best." She sipped a little more coffee, then turned her clear blue eyes on him. "Do you have any children?"

"No. I've never wanted them." *Until I met you.* The sentence popped into his head, startling him with its suddenness. He even wondered if he'd said it aloud. Once more he pushed the thought away as quickly as it came. He was getting real good at that. "So you graduated, had Dee. Then what?"

"I went to beauty school and met Bella and Anna—she was Hollis's mom, she died last year. For some reason the two of them took a liking to me. They used to call me the kid, but they were great. We all worked in the same shop for a while. Then, after my divorce—"

"Divorce? I thought you said—"

"Not Alan. Another guy, later on. My single excursion into wedded bliss," she said dryly. "It lasted less than a year. By the time I filed for divorce, Bella and Anna had opened the two shops, Annabella and Annabella Deux."

T. R. was still mulling over the existence of an ex-husband, but he said, "I get it. Anna and Bella—Annabella."

"Bless them both. I was desperate for a job, and they gave me one. I thought it would be temporary, a stopgap kind of thing." She smiled. "I've been there ever since."

"Did you ever hear from Alan?"

"I ran into him a few years back when a girlfriend and I went up to Lake Tahoe. He was bald, married, and sold insurance. He didn't even ask me about Dee, and you know what? I didn't want to tell him a thing about her anyway. Still, it would have been nice if she'd had a father all those years."

"I'll bet there are a lot of guys who wouldn't have minded being her stepfather. I'm surprised you never married again—surely you've had other opportunities?"

Kate didn't know how to answer him. How to explain that she'd never felt right about any of the men she'd dated over the years. Never felt close, connected, never felt like she could be herself.

The way she did now.

"Do you know what you're doing?" she asked.

"Getting too personal?"

"Getting me to talk about a lot of things I haven't talked about in years, and that I had no intention of talking about with you."

He covered her hand with his. It was the first time he'd touched her that evening, and she was startled at the way her skin welcomed him. "Good," he said, rubbing his thumb over her wrist bone, sending tiny tremors up her arm. "I want to know all about you. I want us to be friends, Kate, I really do, whatever else happens." He looked startled at what he had said, then laughed softly. "I can't believe that came out of my mouth. I don't usually think of women as my friends."

"Then I'm honored," she said lightly. Flustered by her body's shimmering reaction to his touch, she withdrew her hand from his and picked up the menu. It was made up in the style of a four-page newspaper, matching the old French newsprint that covered the restaurant's walls. "I'm also hungry. I haven't eaten much all week, since I . . ." Her voice trailed out weakly.

"—left Hawaii," he said, finishing her sentence and adding quietly, "Neither have I."

It remained hanging in the air—the first mention of that night they'd spent together, and how unsettled, how off balance, both of them had been since. Kate didn't want to talk about that right now, so she studied the menu with intense concentration, aware that T. R. was studying her with the same intensity.

After they each ordered salads, hamburgers, and fries, T. R. added, "And bring a Café Figaro for the lady."

"No," she protested, laughing. "It's too much."

"You said it sounded good. I insist."

"Pushy, aren't you? Okay. I'll have one if you will."

"Make that two, heavy on the chocolate."

They were still grinning at each other when the waiter took off with their orders. "You're devious, you know that?" she said.

"How?"

"I always think I'm stating, very firmly, what I do and do not want. But somehow I wind up doing what *you* want. How do you manage that?"

"Easy. We want the same things. You just take a little longer to get to it, that's all."

The piercing blue eyes that met hers contained just a suggestion of banked fires beneath their amused, perceptive surface. Oh, yes, T. R. understood her very well, and what they were talking about had nothing to do with ordering a drink. He was in control of the situation. She might fight this thing between them, he was saying, but she'd lose. Or should it be called winning?

She drew in a breath, shivering. "Who are you?"

He ran the back of his knuckles over her cheek, just once, then dropped his hand back onto the table. "Just a man, that's all."

"You make me feel . . ."

"What, Kate, what do I make you feel?"

"Like I'm on the edge of a cliff. Scared to go over, scared to stay put."

"Yeah, I know."

"Do you?"

"Sure. I feel things with you that I'm not used to feeling. I don't let myself. I have no idea what's going on here, but you're not alone when you say you're scared." With a rueful snicker, he added, "That's something else I've never admitted to a woman before."

So, as powerful an effect as he had on her, she had the same effect on him. Her heart lightened at the thought. From the beginning, she'd had him pegged as cocky and confident in all his dealings with women. "Do you mean that you've never been serious about anyone?"

He smiled. "My turn for the hot seat, huh?" He lifted his shoulders in a casual shrug. "Not for longer than a couple of months. It's been hard, traveling all the time."

"Where to?"

"All over. I've been around the world twice, and I've seen the backstage of every major concert hall in the United States. One of these days I'd like to return to all the cities I played and really see the sights—not just glimpse them from a bus on its way to the next town."

"I've always thought traveling was exciting."

"That kind of traveling gets old real quick."

"Were you lonely on the road?"

"I think I was, but I was too busy to think about it. I never have been real introspective." Leaning back in his chair, he let a corner of his mouth turn up. "Come on, ask me more."

"Father?"

"He's dead."

"I'm sorry."

"It's been a while. What else?"

"Okay, why did you choose the piano?"

"It chose me. I was just drawn to it, to all keyboards. I tried the bass for a while, because girls seemed to gravitate to bass players, but it didn't do it for me."

" 'Piano Man,' " Kate said. "Billy Joel."

"Good tune."

As they smiled at each other with easy familiarity, Kate felt as if she were meeting T. R. for the first time . . . and that she'd known him forever. "Tell me," she said, "how did we spend all that time together in Hawaii and find out so little about each other?"

He peered at her through half-lidded eyes. "We had other things on our mind."

She nodded, remembering. "I guess we did. So, now that that's been taken care of, we can talk."

One ebony eyebrow rose questioningly. "Are you sure *that*'s been taken care of?"

She was saved from answering him when the salads were put down in front of them. Chewing mindlessly, Kate tried to keep her mind a blank, because when she thought about how T. R.'s mouth had curved suggestively, how his vivid blue eyes had glittered with amusement—and sensuality—as he looked at her, how he'd let down the self-possessed barrier he presented to the world, she found her head all messed up again.

His power, his magnetism, were all the more potent for being understated. She watched his hands as he ate, and even the sight of those long, graceful fingers, which brought back memories of how he'd pleasured her and how the very core of her being had melted for him, was a major distraction.

"Would you like some of my salad?"

"Huh?" Kate looked up. T. R. was pointing to her plate.

"You demolished that one in record time. You really are hungry."

"I told you, starving."

"Here come the burgers. That should fix it."

As she was pouring a liberal amount of ketchup on hers, T. R. said offhandedly, "Tell me about your marriage. When was it?"

"Are we back on me again?"

"This is the last one. Promise."

She took a bite—it was heavenly, and she really was famished—then chewed carefully and swallowed before she answered him. "When Dee was two, I met an older man, a musician, amazingly enough. John Rizzoli. Do you know him?" When he shook his head, she went on, "He said he was crazy about me and my daughter. My mother couldn't stand him, by the way, but he swept me off my feet and took us both with him to Las Vegas."

"Don't tell me—he played in a band at one of the casinos."

"Trumpet at the Sahara."

T. R. popped a fry into his mouth. "That's the problem, you know. First a trombonist, then a trumpet player. You should have stayed away from the brass section."

"Now he tells me. I really tried to make that marriage work—more for Dee's sake, I think, than for my own. After a year, I'd had it with his drinking and little extramarital flings, so I packed us up and came back to L.A. I moved in with Mom and Dad. Then—" Sighing, she patted around her mouth again with her napkin. "Boy, parts of my life sound like a script for a soap opera."

He took another generous bite from his hamburger. "Go on."

"Dad died right after we got back. Heart attack, out of nowhere. Mom fell apart, then she got sick.

She'd always had weak lungs, but they finally diagnosed the emphysema. She couldn't really work full time anymore. So there was Dee to raise and Mom to take care of, and I guess I put my dreams aside and worked as hard as I could. And that's how it's been ever since. End of my story."

"Hey, T. R.!" A young man with very blond hair but dark brown roots came rushing up to the table. A gold cross hung from his left earlobe, and he wore a sleeveless vest over a bare, extremely skinny chest. "Hey, man, long time no see!"

T. R. did a complicated handshake with the newcomer, who pulled a chair over to their table and sat himself down. "Sal," T. R. said. "Good to see you."

"When did you blow into town, and what are you up to?"

"Hanging out, mostly."

"Been jamming at all lately?" Sal asked.

"Here and there. Congratulations on the gold album. You deserved it—the tunes were terrific."

"Hey, you were a big help. I mean, not just sitting in on the sessions, but you got my head straightened out before I completely blew it."

T. R. shrugged, looking slightly uncomfortable with his friend's gratitude. "No big deal. I knew what you were going through, that's all. Takes one to know one."

Sal nodded, then seemed to notice Kate for the first time. "Well, well," he said, giving her a thorough once-over. "Hey, I didn't mean to, you know, interrupt or anything." He beamed a big smile at Kate, revealing a gold tooth in the middle of a lot of white ones.

"Kate O'Brien, this is Salvador Dolly."

Kate looked at T. R. to see if he was putting her on. He wasn't. "Hey, Kate, nice to meet you," Sal said. He winked at T. R. "You always did get the lookers."

Deciding that this was supposed to be a compliment, she smiled back. "Nice to meet you."

"Yeah. Well, listen," Sal said, rising. "I gotta go. Gimme a call, okay? I'm still up in the hills. Maybe we can jam. Later."

As Sal took off, two giggling teenage girls stopped him and asked for an autograph, one on her wrist, the other on her bare midriff. Their requests granted, they left, still giggling.

"Salvador Dalí?" Kate said suspiciously, taking a swig of her chocolate drink. "Like the painter?"

"D—O—L—L—Y. His real name is Francis Dooley."

"I see. Should I know him? Will Dee be impressed if I say I met him?"

T. R. crossed his hands behind his head and looked amused. "He's pretty big, hit the top of the charts twice last year."

"Boy, I'm really out of it. When I was a kid, I knew the name and birthday of every member of the bands I liked."

"Heavy metal? Punk?"

"Uh-uh, never. Soft rock, some folk. Dee says my taste is one step up from elevator music."

He laughed. "I knew you weren't perfect."

"Is that the kind of music you play—like your friend? You know, purple hair, and leather and chains?"

"I used to."

"I'm glad I didn't know you then." Kate picked up her hamburger and took another bite, then wiped some ketchup off the corner of her mouth. "He treated you like some kind of mentor."

"I just helped him get off drugs. He was freebasing, really strung out, and I told him my story. He says it helped him get straight. Not a big deal."

"Your story?"

"I used to do a lot of the heavy stuff. There was a time when I couldn't have told you the day or the town or the year . . . or my name. I'm real lucky to be alive."

"I had no idea."

"I've been clean for years."

"Good for you."

"It was stop or die."

She frowned. "You say that so casually."

"I don't mean it that way. I just don't want to get melodramatic. You know"—he smiled ruefully—"it's not cool."

Kate looked down, her fingernail tracing some initials that had long ago been carved on the old, scarred table. "What you just told me terrifies me."

"Why?"

"Dee. She thinks she wants the life you've led. All of it. What if she goes out there and gets just as lost as you did?"

"Not *everyone* gets lost," he said gently. "But you can't control the way Dee spends her life, Kate. No one can. If she's got music in her, she has to go after it. She may have a couple of rough years ahead of her, I'll grant you that. But if she's as solid as I think she is, she'll come out of it just fine."

"I wish I could be as calm about her as you are, but you're not her mother."

"I know."

Kate shook herself out of her mood with a self-mocking smile. "I feel so innocent. Besides a little experimenting in high school, my total experience with mood-altering substances has been to have a couple of glasses of wine and go to sleep."

"Stay that way, *querida*."

Her breath stopped, and she had difficulty swallowing the food she'd been chewing.

He'd called her *querida*. It brought it all back. All the magic of that night under the stars, in his arms. Her body remembered instantly, with soft, tingling sensations all up and down, and inside, too, where she wanted to feel him again, filling her, making her complete. She took another long drink from her Café Figaro, then licked the foam from around her mouth. She was scared at how needy she felt, needy for T. R.

T. R. saw Kate's face change and knew that she was remembering the night he had never forgotten. When her tongue moved over her lips, he groaned silently, wanting her with an intensity that burned him to a crisp. It had been like this since they'd met on the beach, he thought, gazing at that impossibly lovely face that had been made stronger by age and experience.

He wondered what the hell he was going to do about her.

This evening wasn't going at all the way he planned. He'd intended to pin her down about why she'd split that night in Hawaii, then do his best to ensure a repeat performance. He was staying at a hotel but using a musician buddy's office on Sunset Strip to work on the film score. The office had a nice little couch that made up into a bed, and he'd wanted very much to get Kate into that bed as soon after dinner as possible.

Instead, they were playing "Getting to Know You," sharing parts of their lives with each other. He was telling her things he barely admitted to himself, let alone a woman. It felt . . . intimate. Intimate was for when he was making music, not when he was with a woman.

As far back as he could remember, T. R. had tamped down any feelings of tenderness when a woman threatened to become too important. He'd used his music, his ambition, then drugs and alcohol to keep as far from romantic entanglements as possible. But somehow Kate had subtly undermined his usual defensive barriers; he felt himself moving closer and closer to wanting, needing, *loving*, this woman with an intensity that was unlike anything he'd ever felt.

Even when he was making music.

She fiddled nervously with her food for a few moments, then pushed the plate away. "Well, I'm done."

"No dessert?"

She patted her stomach. "Are you kidding? I'm stuffed. Also tired. I'd better get home."

"Take a little walk with me first. It's a beautiful night."

She didn't want to leave yet, either, he realized, and he felt ridiculously happy when she said, "Okay, but just for a few minutes. I have to get up pretty early."

After T. R. paid the bill, they went through the noisy room and out onto Melrose, where a hot August night had completely taken over the summer sky. No stars were visible, and the air felt close, but not humid. The heat melted Kate's bones; she felt surprisingly relaxed. When T. R. took her hand, she felt giddy, like a young girl on her first date. Neither of them spoke for a while as they passed other after-dinner strollers and rows of storefronts displaying antiques, furniture, and jewelry.

"Dinner was nice," he said finally.

"Yes."

"So is this." He squeezed her hand gently. "Being with you."

"Yes." She felt . . . happy.

After another companionable silence, T. R. said, "Tell me about your dreams."

"What?"

"Earlier you said you had to put your dreams aside when your dad died. What are they?"

"You have an amazing memory."

"It's my ear—when I hear a tune once, I can play it. The same with words. Tell me."

Stopping, she turned to look at a window display of Tiffany-style lamps. In the glass she could see herself and T. R. side by side, hand in hand. "I don't have dreams anymore."

"Bull."

Smiling, she said, "Yeah, you're right. Okay. I'd like to go back to school, get a college education. I'd like to travel. I'm dying to go to Florence and see everything Michelangelo ever created. I want to take an art class, a music appreciation class, and read a lot of books that I'm too tired at night to read. I want to do a lot of things that take free time, and money, and more energy than I have."

He brought her hand up to his mouth and kissed her palm lightly. "See? You remember your dreams."

"Sure, but I have to stay in reality. There's a couple of very special people depending on me."

In the glass he was looking at her with an uncharacteristically gentle expression, as if he wanted to say something. She turned her gaze on him. "What are you thinking about?"

"You, when I first knew you, and you now. Me then, me now. How we've changed. How much we're the same. Come."

Still holding her hand, he angled them down a tree-lined side street and continued walking. Kate was feeling peaceful, but she didn't know why. Nothing had really been settled. "Somehow, I did most of the talking tonight," she said.

"There'll be other nights."

"Will there?"

"Yes." He sounded so sure.

"Remember George in Hawaii? Well, I keep thinking I need someone like him."

"Give me a break." T. R. shook his head. "No way. George was too straight for you."

"What do you mean?"

He stopped and, putting his hands on her shoulders, turned her to him. "You'd be miserable with a button-down guy like him—they're too predictable."

"You think so? Knowing what someone was going to do before he did it? I'd love it."

T. R. smiled into her eyes, but he wasn't buying it.

"A guy like that doesn't run out on you when you're pregnant," she went on. "And he doesn't screw around and make you feel like dirt. He comes home when he says he's coming home. He plans ahead. You know you can count on him."

Again, his expression was gently compassionate. "Hey, you had a couple of bad experiences, that's all. Not every man—hell, not every musician—is like those two were." He smoothed her cheek with his fingertips and added softly, "I'm not like that."

She felt herself shuddering on an indrawn breath, wondering why she had a sudden urge to lean her head against the soft cotton of his shirt and feel his strong, comforting arms around her. In the next moment his sapphire eyes, the firm, full mouth, his very presence, drew her upper body toward him like half of a high-powered magnet. She smelled a faint, not unpleasant, aroma of male perspiration mixed with lemon after-shave. She felt her lids lowering, her body swaying toward his, when two men walked by, staring at them and laughing softly.

The intrusion startled her out of the moment. Turning away so that T. R.'s hands dropped from her shoulders, Kate began to walk again.

After a moment he came up next to her. "Do I frighten you?"

"I guess you do, a little. I guess that's why predictability seems so desirable."

"Tell me something, Kate O'Brien," he said easily. "The world is full of bean counters with neat desks—they're all over the place. So like I asked you before, in all these years, why haven't you married one of them?"

She thought about it, then shook her head. "I don't know. I honestly don't know."

Neither she nor T. R. spoke again until they reached her aging little compact. After she unlocked it, she leaned against the car door, looking down while she twisted her keys in her hands. At sometime during the evening, her staunch opposition to this man had abated to where it was now only a token resistance. She wasn't quite ready to surrender—but the urge to do so was so strong that it scared her.

T. R. rested an elbow against the door, at the side of her head. As his body brushed hers, she felt her breath catch in her throat.

"Kate."

"What?" They both whispered in the warm, deserted street.

"I want to see you. I'll be here for another week, and I'll be pretty busy, but I want to be with you."

She fiddled with her keys. "For another week. And then what?" she couldn't help adding.

Leaning closer, he brushed her ear with his lips. "Then we see what happens."

"Look, T. R." She tried to sound reasonable, but feeling his warm breath on her neck made it difficult. "I came here tonight because you said I owed you an explanation."

Velvet lips nibbled along her cheekbone line. "Which I haven't heard."

"Huh?"

"Why did you run out on me?"

Against her will, she found her eyes closing. His lips swept across first one lid, then the other. "Because it was too wonderful."

She heard him chuckle softly. "It was wonderful, so you had to run away?"

"It made sense at the time." Now his mouth trailed slowly down her cheek toward her mouth. She had to give it one last try. "You said earlier, no matter what happened, we could be friends. Can we—?"

T. R. never let Kate get the rest of the sentence out because he brought his hands up to either side of her head, imprisoning her body with his, and kissed her, very slowly and thoroughly. Even as she gasped with surprise, her lips parted for him automatically so his tongue could explore and taste every millimeter of her soft, honeyed mouth.

He made sure the kiss went on for what seemed a breathless eternity. Then he released his hold and pulled back to look at her. She stared at him through eyes glazed with passion, breathing with quick, light gasps that made her breasts move up and down through her shirt.

Ignoring the sudden painful hardening between his legs, he carefully moved her away from the car, opened the door, and helped her into the driver's seat. Then he pried the keys from her hand, put them in the ignition, rolled down the window, and closed and locked the door. Leaning on the door-frame, an inch from her startled face, he offered her the most reassuring smile he could.

"There's more to me than you know, Kate O'Brien," he whispered. "I am already your friend. And I am already in your life, whether you admit it or not, and whether you like it or not. Get used to me."

He stepped away and leaned against the tree once more.

"Now, go home and get some sleep, *querida*. I'll call you tomorrow."

Eight

All the next day at work, as she listened with one ear for T. R.'s call, Kate couldn't keep her mind from dwelling on the question he'd raised the night before. Why hadn't she managed—in all these years—to find a straight-arrow type and settle down with him? Most women with a young child and invalid mother would have made it a priority to ensure that there was a man around the house. It wasn't as if she had a big agenda against all men, after all, just those whose lifestyle made them untrustworthy partners. So, what was it? Why had she found fault with every man she'd dated for any length of time? What had she been looking for?

Whom had she been waiting for?

Her heart stopped every time the phone rang, but as Friday stretched on and T. R. didn't call, she found her spirits flagging and depression setting in. Maybe that closeness they'd felt last night had scared him as much as it scared her. Maybe he'd decided to back off. Maybe that incredible good-night kiss had been a good-bye kiss.

Just as she finished applying the top coat to her

last client's nails, the phone rang, and she knew it was him. Her heart pounded with excitement as she picked up the receiver. "Annabella, how may I help you?"

"If I thought you really meant that," T. R. said with a smile in his voice, "I'd have a few suggestions."

She had a smile of her own for him. "Subtle, aren't you?"

"When it comes to you, not very. Are you busy with someone?"

"Just finished." Kate moved out of the manicurist's straight-backed chair and settled into the comfortable, cushioned one where her customers sat.

"How are you today?" he asked.

"Tired."

"Yeah, me too. I had a little trouble sleeping last night."

She smiled again into the phone. "Tell me about it."

"I wish you were with me right now."

"Where are you?"

"In a little studio that belongs to a buddy of mine, off Sunset Strip. It's kind of a dump, but with a lot of character. At night, from my window, I can see all the kids and cars cruising along the boulevard. Behind me, there's all those lights in the hills, and beyond those, the ocean." He let out a mirthless chuckle. "Not that I can see the ocean, of course. This damned L.A. smog doesn't make it easy to see anything. But the water's there, and I know it. And I like it."

His voice was mesmerizing, and she loved listening to it—that mellow sound with faint echoes of his Mexican heritage. "What are you doing there?"

"Making up some tunes."

"I didn't know you were a composer."

"Too fancy a word for what I do. But, yeah, I've been getting into it lately. I'm scoring a film, my first one."

"Really? That's exciting."

"If I don't screw it up, yeah." He said it lightly, but she detected a slightly forlorn note, a touch of fear in his voice. She wished she were with him right then.

"Why didn't you tell me about this last night?"

"We covered a lot. No way we could get to it all. Look, Kate—"

"Yes?"

"I'm way behind on this thing. I'm going to have to pull an all-nighter, I think—"

He was telling her he wouldn't be seeing her; she couldn't believe how much that hurt.

"—so how about Saturday night?"

From being smashed to the ground, her heart took wing; how vulnerable she'd become to him in such a short time. "I get off work about seven."

"Then I'll see you about eight at your house."

"Do you know where I live?"

"I remember. I never forgot."

"All right." She felt like laughing out loud, but there were still a couple of customers who were busybodies in the shop, and she didn't want to attract their attention.

"And Kate, on Saturday?"

"Yes?"

"Spend the night with me. Please."

"Yes," she said.

She realized that he'd been holding his breath because he let it out on a soft, grateful sigh. "Good. I'll leave you with this."

She heard the phone being set down, then the sound of T. R. playing a melody on the piano. It started out simply, a wistful little air, but he added some complicated chords, and the simple tune wound up in an emotional, soaring crescendo.

"That's beautiful," Kate said.

"Yeah, well." He didn't take compliments gracefully, either, she observed. "See you Saturday, *querida*."

After he hung up, T. R. couldn't wipe the grin off his face. He found his fingers roaming over the piano keys, noodling some more and coming up with variations on that melody he'd played over the phone. It *was* a catchy tune, if he said so himself, and would serve as the lovers' theme throughout the whole film, whenever the hero and heroine were together.

On the score, the melody had the title: Cue 116. But to T. R., it would always be known as Kate's Theme.

"It's me, Mom," Kate called out, wincing as the screen door slammed loudly. That new automatic-close hinge wasn't adjusted quite right; she'd get to it this weekend.

"I'm in the dining room, dear," came her mother's raspy voice.

Rifling quickly through the pile of bills on the small table by the front door, Kate turned into the alcove they called a dining room but that was barely large enough to seat six. "Where's Dee?"

"Out with Ronnie."

On one corner of the table sat a huge pile of chartreuse leaflets and envelopes. Claire O'Brien, thin, gray-haired, and at fifty-five looking ten years older, was dwarfed by the pile. "What's this?" Kate asked.

"Fliers from the new shoe outlet in the mall. I told them I'd have them stuffed and ready to go by Monday morning." With her emphysema, Claire couldn't hold a full-time job, so she undertook various at-home projects that didn't pay much, but certainly helped. Without breaking the rhythm of her folding and stuffing, she smiled warmly at her daughter.

Kate kissed her mother's head, catching a glimpse of herself in the wall mirror above the ancient sideboard. She looked as tired as she felt, which made sense—sleep had been eluding her as of late. But she also noticed a glow about her, as though she were lit from inside by a candle.

Pulling the rubber band out of her hair and scratching her scalp, she said, "Ronnie again?"

"They're just friends, Kate, or so Dee has explained. There are boyfriends and there are boy *friends.* Ronnie is a boy *friend.*"

"Who happens to have a driver's license and a car. Dee isn't stupid. Where'd they go?"

"To the movies, then to a coffeehouse to hear a guitarist, I think. She also mentioned something about dancing."

"She'll be home by midnight?"

"She promised."

"Okay."

Claire looked at her daughter with a mixture of amusement and exasperation. "You've been riding her pretty hard lately, Kate."

Her mother usually tried not to interfere with the way Kate raised Dee, so when Claire said something like this, Kate knew she should pay attention. Leaning a hip against the table, she said thoughtfully, "Have I? I don't mean to. Why, has she been complaining?"

"Not really. It's just hard being a grandmother and seeing the two of you circle around each other. It's a difficult age, I know that."

Kate smiled wryly. "Mine or hers?"

"Both. What are you so worried about?"

"Her hormones are finally checking in—that's a dangerous time. Remember?"

Claire shrugged philosophically. "Dee knows about safe sex and how we feel about waiting till she's older. There's not much you can do about hormones, Kate. Like there's not much you can do about Dee—she's mostly formed by now."

That's funny," Kate said as she sat on a faded upholstered chair across from her mother, "T. R. made a comment very much like that last night."

"Who's this T. R.?" Claire looked up from her pile

of leaflets. "Dee hasn't stopped talking about him this past week."

"A man I met in Hawaii. A musician."

"Oh," Claire said. "That's why she hasn't stopped talking about him. Is there anything else you want me to know?"

Kate felt an overwhelming rush of love for her mother—for her wisdom and her tact. And her solid presence throughout all the difficult years past. "I'm going out with him tomorrow night."

"Oh?"

"And by the end of the week, he'll be leaving L.A."

"Oh." After assessing her daughter's face and nodding, Claire went back to her task.

Leaning an elbow on the table, Kate rested her chin in her hand and said wistfully, "Dee's not my little girl anymore, is she? I miss her."

"The way I missed you when you started growing up. It's a passage, like they say in the magazines. Both of us should probably have had more kids."

"But we didn't." Kate pushed herself up from the table. "Let me wash up and grab a bite, and then I'll help you with that pile."

Kate pulled up in front of the house with a squeal of tires, then dashed inside. It was nearly eight-thirty on Saturday night, and she'd wanted to be home an hour ago to clean up and get beautiful for T. R. A dead battery had taken care of that. An hour had been wasted while the man at the corner gas station kept saying he'd be with her in a moment. She'd tried to call home but kept getting a busy signal. Dee, of course. Maybe it was time to give her daughter her own phone, as Dee had repeatedly requested.

Kate had finally gotten through just as T. R. was pulling up outside her house, and she'd asked her mother to entertain him till she got there.

Now, as she stood in the living room entryway, she noted that T. R. was ensconced in the only comfortable chair in the house, his feet up on the ottoman, a cold drink in his hand. He wore a midnight-blue cotton sweater over faded jeans, and once again Kate was struck by how very masculine, how unconventional, his beauty was. And how at home he was in his own body. And what a body it was. Tonight she would get to see it again, to touch it, to feel him inside her. As she'd been doing all day, she found herself shivering with excitement at the thought of spending a whole night with him, wrapped in his arms.

Sitting on either side of T. R. were Dee and Claire, obviously hanging on to every word he was saying. He looked like a king, Kate thought with a smile, holding court. Or a sultan with his adoring harem.

"Sorry I'm late," she said as she folded her arms and leaned against the wall. "But you don't seem to be suffering too badly."

He put down his drink and rose from his chair. She walked over to him. "Hi," he said, kissing her on the cheek.

When he pulled back so she could see him close up, she frowned. "You look awful."

"Gracious, as always."

"Seriously," she continued. He had dark circles under his lower lids, and the whites of his eyes were anything but white. His golden skin tone was paler than usual, as though he'd been deprived of sun for a long time. Kate was concerned, but as both her mother and daughter were in the room, she fought down the urge to brush a few stray strands of his hair off his forehead. "Are you all right, T. R.? I mean, are you sick or something?"

"Just tired, and you can stop fussing. I'm not going to pass out."

She put her hands on her waist and glared at him. "How long has it been since you slept?"

"A while," he said with a lazy smile. "I used to be able to stay up three days in a row with no problem, but I was younger then."

Placing her hand on his chest, Kate pushed him back down onto the armchair. Then she seated herself on the ottoman and peered at him anxiously. "We're staying here tonight," she announced. "How does pizza sound to everyone?"

T. R. laughed, momentarily reversing the direction of the downward, weary lines in his face. "Hey, I haven't seen this side of you yet."

"What side?"

"Mother hen. Cluck-cluck-cluck."

"Are you kidding?" Dee exclaimed. "She's the worst! She worries all the time!"

"Dee," chided Claire. "You know that's not true."

"I'm sorry," said Kate, wondering suddenly if she'd overstepped her bounds. "I didn't mean to—"

"That's okay." Lifting his hand, he waved away her apology. "It's been a while since anyone worried about me. I kind of like it." The look he gave her was softly intimate, unspoken but potent with meaning. She returned his gaze and smiled, feeling overwhelmed by a strong surge of emotion, one that she was reluctant to name.

She knew whatever it was was written all over her face so that Claire and Dee could see it. But it didn't matter if they did. This was all for her. She owned it. She deserved it.

"Mom," Dee said. "T. R.'s been telling us about this film score he's working on. It's a movie for television. Isn't that cool?"

Kate, still caught up in T. R.'s silent communication, nodded. "Very cool."

"And I told T. R. about the concert me and Dave and Rhino are giving on Friday night." She turned to T. R. and asked eagerly, "Do you think you'll be able to come? Maybe, like, give us a few pointers?"

He turned to the bright-eyed teenager. "I don't know, Dee. That's the day of the full orchestra session. I will if I can, but don't count on it."

"See, Mom? T. R.'s going to try to come to my concert!"

Kate looked at her daughter's shining face, filled with expectation and youth and hope, and her own euphoria vanished. Don't make it too important, she wanted to say. Like the man said, don't count on it. Your heart might get broken.

And then she wondered just who the advice was meant for.

"So, I told him that he might bloody well think the nude is offensive," Hollis said with fervor, "but I think it's magnificent, and as long as this gallery reflects my taste, the nude stays."

Bella frowned. "I admire your spunk, Hollis, but can this man make any trouble for us?"

"Tony says he hasn't a legal leg to stand on."

Kate was listening to her two friends with only part of her brain. Fiery Hollis was on another of her "art" high horses, all about freedom of expression. Bella, who was Hollis's partner in both the Annabellas and the new gallery next door, was a bit more diplomatic by nature, not to mention fifteen years older.

The three of them were having their traditional once-a-month Sunday dinner, indulging in girl talk—which often translated into talk about men—and anything else that crossed their minds. There was nothing of a spicy nature from Bella, a widow who never went out. And Kate's social life had been bleak the past couple of years.

Hollis had dominated the dinners for a few months, filled with plans for her new gallery and her new marriage to Tony Stellini, Carla's ex-husband. Hollis fairly glowed with love, and while Kate was happy for her friend, she also secretly envied her.

Kate picked a piece of shrimp out of her paella;

this month's restaurant was a Spanish one. "You're so lucky," she sighed.

"That I am," said Hollis, "but to what subject in particular are you referring?"

"Tony."

"Why, Kate, I didn't know you coveted my husband."

"Don't be a twit," Kate said, smiling as she imitated Hollis's musical accent. "It's just nice that you have someone dependable like that—you know, a lawyer with a steady paycheck and normal hours."

Hollis raised one eyebrow. "There's nothing normal about Tony Stellini, and you know it. He's impossibly arrogant, obsessed with his work, and given to lecturing me. He's also outrageously extravagant, so it's a good thing we don't have to live on his steady paycheck."

Bella put her hand on Kate's arm. "Kate," she said gently, "you've had a long face all evening. What is it?"

"Does it have anything to do with that lovely man with two initials for a name?" asked Hollis. "I must say, I rather liked him myself."

"Have you seen him lately?" Bella asked.

"Thursday night. And last night."

"Seriously?"

"Have you been keeping this a secret?" Hollis gave Kate an admonishing look. "You traitor. Don't we have an agreement to discuss all men that come into our lives? Didn't you wrench every detail of Tony's and my courtship out of me?"

"This is different. It's not a courtship, by a long shot. It's . . ." She sighed audibly, then laughed. "I don't know what it is. Sort of an affair, only he's in the middle of a big project, and it's been difficult getting together." T. R. had fallen asleep on her couch last night. Then, after Claire had stuffed him with a huge breakfast, he'd left to go back to his studio to work.

So much for fantasies about all-night lovemaking.

"Sounds fascinating," said Hollis. "Tell us all about it."

"I don't know what to say. I'm going to need both of you when it's over, though."

"Why are you talking about it being over? It's barely begun."

Kate shrugged and played with the saffron rice on her plate. "T. R.'s the kind of man I've been avoiding all my life. Too restless ever to be happy in one place. Undependable income. Weird friends. He's always traveling, never stays anywhere for long. He can't be what I need, and I've been around long enough to know you can't change someone's nature. So there's no future."

Kate looked up into the concerned faces of her two dear friends. "Thank you both for being here and listening. I haven't talked about this to anyone, and it's been weighing on me."

"We love you," Bella said warmly, squeezing her hand.

"Ditto," Hollis said. "But about the traveling and the restlessness, Kate—that could be fun."

Bella, ever the optimist, added, "Of course. In another two years Dee will be off to college, and you can go with him."

"How can I? What about Mom?"

"She's been talking about living with your aunt Tress for years," Bella pointed out. "And you don't need her to watch Dee anymore while you're at work. You can finally have some freedom."

"All well and good, but you're forgetting one thing," Kate said sardonically. "He hasn't asked me, and I don't expect him to. He told me his relationships never last more than a couple of months. Of course," she added, "he's also told me that he feels things with me he's never felt before."

"There. You see?" Hollis said.

As Bella's warm brown eyes met Kate's she nodded slowly. "You're in love with him, aren't you?"

"Of course not. I *can't* be, can I?" She tried to swallow a sudden thick lump in her throat. "Oh, I don't know anything—except that I feel like crying."

"Oh, Kate, don't." Hollis's lower lip trembled as she took her napkin and wiped moisture from her lower lid.

"I hate to see you like this." Bella's eyes, too, had filled.

The three women looked at each other for a long, sad moment, each thinking about the pain of love instead of the joy. "Don't, you two," Kate said finally. "I don't want to feel any worse than I already do."

"Well then," Hollis said, "what are you going to do about this T. R. bloke?"

"Be with him as much as I can, I guess," Kate answered, stabbing halfheartedly at a piece of chicken. "He'll be gone soon, and everything will be back to normal."

"If you say so," said Hollis with a dubious look at Bella.

"Dee," Kate called out as she came down the stairs, "fix me an espresso, will you?" It was just before five o'clock on Wednesday, one of the two afternoons that Dee helped out at Annabella Deux. It was Kate's habit to grab a quick demitasse and visit with her daughter before the last appointment of the day.

As she reached the last stair, the long pine bar that served as a counter came into view. It was loaded with items from various sections of the shop. There were several of the potpourri-filled pillows in assorted colors, beeswax candles, an open-weave blanket from Ireland, and at least twenty bars of imported soap wrapped in gaily colored tissue paper. There were no customers in the shop that Kate could see.

"Hello there." T. R. came out from the tiny room that housed a display of miniature pillboxes and picture frames. He wore his hair in a low ponytail and had on tight jeans and a scoop-neck, sleeveless orange T-shirt that revealed every sleekly muscled inch of his arms and chest. "These too, Dee," he said, smiling at Kate and adding one silver frame and two porcelain boxes to the other items.

"What's all this?" Kate asked, poised on the step.

Dee appeared with an armful of the shop's silver wrapping paper. "T. R.'s buying a bunch of stuff, Mom."

"So I see."

Dee disappeared again—for more paper, probably—and Kate wondered if T. R. could hear how loudly and rapidly her heart was beating. The sight of him left her breathless. It always did, it seemed. She hadn't seen him for three days, since Sunday morning; they spoke on the phone several times a day, but his film score had proved to be even more taxing than he'd expected.

"I needed to pick up some gifts," he said, "and I remembered all the great stuff from when I was here before."

She wanted to ask him who the gifts were for, but that might sound as if she were prying, or even jealous.

She wanted to ask if he knew how much his pile of goodies would cost, but suddenly she realized she had no idea what kind of money he earned as a musician and that such a question might sound condescending.

She wanted to ask how his composing was coming along. And how did he get his jeans to fit like that? And where was he off to when the week was up?

And was he as hungry for her as she was for him?

"I'm done, Kate." T. R. walked over to the stair
way and leaned on the banister. Excitement and
triumph radiated from those incredible blue eyes
of his. "The score is at the copyist's, the sessions
are tomorrow and Friday, and today I'm a free man.
Free." He lowered his voice. "So, what do you think,
querida? Want to be with me tonight?"

Did she ever! Kate felt her mouth curve upward.
Her tongue formed a positive reply to his invitation
but a little imp that lived in her and sometimes
came out at the oddest times chose that moment
to make an appearance. "Sorry. I'm busy," she said,
sauntering past him and over to the bar.

She went behind the counter and began the
process of making espresso. "Would you like a cap
puccino or an espresso? We also have cookies and
biscuits, if you'd like."

She felt rather than saw T. R. staring at her back;
the heat from his gaze was probably burning a hole
through her blouse. She stirred the small spoon in
her cup. Turning slowly, she leaned on the counter, knowing that the V-neck blouse she was wearing today would drape open slightly, affording him
a small glimpse of what was beneath.

"See anything you like?" she said, looking up at
him through lowered lids.

His reaction to her question—the flaring nostrils,
the amused smile, the coiled intensity under the
seemingly casual demeanor—was as familiar, as
dear, to her as if she had known him her whole
life. "You," he said softly. "I'll take one of you."

"Are these on a credit card, T. R.?" Dee's entrance
made Kate shelve her planned reply until a more
appropriate time, when she and T. R. were alone.

"Well, my five o'clock should be here at any
moment," Kate said cheerfully. " 'Bye." And with
an innocent little wave, she came out from behind
the counter and started back up the stairs to the
nail salon.

T. R. watched Kate's retreating back, fighting

down a sudden urge to laugh out loud. She was playing hard to get, not seriously, of course. Not very, anyway. She was probably punishing him for being unavailable all week, especially after he'd announced his intentions to take up a lot of her time.

He'd been as disappointed as she was, but it couldn't be helped; until he was more experienced and more confident, writing notes on a page would go slowly. Maybe he and Kate could have met for an hour or two, but T. R. wanted the next time with her to last a lot longer than that. Hell, had he known Kate O'Brien was about to be in his life, he would have postponed his debut as a composer for a while.

He took out his wallet and handed a credit card to Dee. "Take care of this, will you? And wrap them any way you want. Wait. How will I know what's in each package?"

"I'll put little stickum notes on each one, okay? Who are they for?"

"Mostly for your mother. But don't tell her I said that."

He took the stairs two at a time. When he got up to the nail salon, he looked over at Kate's station, but she wasn't there or anywhere else in the room. Others were, however—four manicurists and their clients, all of whom studied him avidly, without any pretense of discretion. He wondered if his fly was unzipped; from the way some of them were giving him the eye, they might not have minded if it was.

He found Kate in the small kitchen in the rear of the salon, perched on the tile counter next to the sink. She didn't seem in the least surprised to see him. He closed the door behind him and looked at her. Her hair was in a high ponytail, and she looked very young, especially with the mischievous grin on her face. She wore brightly colored leggings and sandals and swung her legs back and forth, kicking the counter like a naughty child.

T. R. walked over to her and positioned his body between her legs. Spreading his hands on the tops of her thighs, he rubbed his thumbs back and forth over the thin cotton material. He heard her quick intake of breath; she stopped the movement of her legs. "What's all this about being busy?" he asked.

"I have a previous engagement, one that I can't get out of."

He bent closer and rubbed his nose against the soft, smooth flesh of her neck. "Oh? What is it?"

"An open house for one of my clients." Kate inhaled sharply as he slowly licked around her ear at the same time his hands crept higher on her thighs. "She just moved into a condo, and she invited me—Oh."

His thumbs curved in at the center of her mound, and he used his nails to scratch lightly at the folds of sensitive flesh beneath the fabric. "Who's the client?"

Kate groaned and threw her head back, thrusting her breasts against his chest. "Carla"—he could feel the tight pebbles of her nipples through his own thin shirt—"Stellini," Kate finished on a gasp.

There was a discreet knock at the door, followed by Bella's voice. "Kate? Mrs. York is here."

"Coming," she called out as she straightened up and hopped off the counter. "Actually," she whispered to him, "I'm just breathing hard."

He pulled her to him and kissed her quickly but thoroughly.

"I'll call Carla and tell her I can't be there," Kate said.

"Don't bother."

"You didn't take me seriously, did you? I do want to see you, you know that."

He grinned. "And you will, *querida*. You will."

Nine

"It's getting late. Are you sure she said she'd come?" T. R. asked.

"Relax." Carla took two glasses of champagne from the tray of a passing server and handed one to him. "She'll be here. She promised. I had to twist her arm, of course, made a big deal of all the years I've been her client and how much it meant to me. But she'll be here."

T. R. glanced around the high-ceilinged room with large windows that overlooked both the San Fernando Valley and downtown. Small groups of beautifully dressed people stood around smiling and chatting, and Carla's taste, which ran to the Santa Fe look, provided a luxurious backdrop: Pale area rugs over hardwood floors, large, comfortable couches, low tables, and woven wall hangings. And in the center of the room, an enormous shiny black baby grand.

"You have a great place," he said. "Thanks for letting me invite myself."

"Hey, for one of Marty's favorite clients, it's my pleasure."

T. R. had recognized Carla Stellini at the nail salon the previous week. She worked at the law firm that represented his interests and was a good friend of Marty Villers, his attorney. After Kate mentioned Carla's open house that night, T. R. arranged to be there.

It was devious, it was about as uncool as you could get, but he wanted to see her face when she walked in. He smiled when he thought of how she'd declared, "Sorry. I'm busy," in that cute, uppity way. He had plans for later this evening that would keep her very busy.

The piano had been drawing him since he'd arrived, so he wandered over to it and sat down. Setting his untouched champagne glass near the music stand, he ran his fingers up and down the keyboard while deciding what to play. Some of his rock buddies would have been horrified, but lately T. R. had gotten really turned on to Gershwin, Cole Porter; the old guys—they really knew how to write a melody. Smiling to himself, he broke into one of his favorites, "Our Love Is Here to Stay."

After handing her shawl to the attendant at the front door, Kate checked her makeup in the hall mirror, pleased to hear the sounds of an old standard coming from Carla's living room. She couldn't have cared less about attending this open house—too many people, too much loud talk and drinking—but she'd promised. It was a good thing someone had invented the cover-up stuff you put under your eyes to mask circles, because without it she wouldn't have made it out the door. Restless and unable to sleep well this whole week, she was sure it showed on her face.

She stepped back and fluffed her hair. The outfit was okay, Kate thought, navy blue pants and bandeau top, with a see-through net cover-up over it.

She had on long blue-and-white ceramic earrings—
Dee had insisted she wear them.

Oh, how she didn't want to be here! She wanted
to be with T. R., who'd pulled a mysterious disap-
pearing act. She supposed that after she got home
this evening, he would call. But what in the world
was he up to?

Taking a deep breath to steel herself, Kate followed the sounds of the piano to the top step of
Carla's sunken living room and looked around.
There were a lot of people there, show-biz types
mostly. Kate was never very comfortable with the
Hollywood set; they seemed to occupy a different
planet, with their self-centered preening and talk
about "the Business" and "deals." Still, she supposed she ought to give the evening a chance.

With the huge piano lid raised, she couldn't
see the face of the player. However, an extremely
well-endowed woman wearing a low-cut sweater
was giving the pianist a flirtatious look, so she
assumed it was a man. Kate smiled sardonically
as he launched into "The Man I Love," another old
favorite that her mother used to sing around the
house. It was one of those waiting-for-a-big-strong-
man-to-take-care-of-me kind of songs.

Fairy tales, Kate thought. Poppycock.

Stepping down into the room, she made her way
around the piano toward the bar, glancing casually
at the pianist.

T. R.

The sight of him stopped her in her tracks. "My
God," she said, and swallowed hard. It was him,
right here in the same room. His eyes were closed,
and his head was bent over the keys, moving gracefully from side to side, as though keeping time with
some rhythm instrument only he could hear.

He was dressed in black—black linen pants into
which was tucked a silk shirt, its sleeves rolled up
and the top three buttons undone, revealing warm
bronze skin. His loose hair partially covered his

face; soft, thick waves swayed with the movement of his head.

Kate put her hand to her breast, as though to keep her wildly beating heart from leaping out of her chest. When a waiter passed by with a tray, she grabbed a glass of champagne, downing at least half of it before coming to her senses and remembering that she didn't hold her liquor very well.

What was T. R. doing here? Was he a guest? Carla had never mentioned knowing him; in fact, she'd even asked Kate who he was. Why hadn't he told her he'd be here? Maybe he was the hired pianist, making some extra money while working on that TV film he'd told her about. He'd said once that musicians never turned down work because they never knew when their next job would turn up. That must be it, she thought. He needed extra money.

While she'd been musing about him, her feet had managed to carry her over to where T. R. sat, lost in his own private world. The woman in the sweater gave Kate the once-over, then smiled dismissively, turning back to T. R. and draping herself across the lid so that her sizable breasts were displayed to their full advantage.

T. R. ignored her, but he seemed to know the moment Kate got to his side. Without any break occurring in his playing, his eyes snapped open, and he looked up at her. Then his mouth curved in that languid, amused smile of his, and he moved over on the bench, indicating that she should sit next to him.

Kate smiled sweetly at the other woman, who huffed and took herself off. Then Kate sank down onto the hard seat, loving her nearness to T. R., the male smell of him, wanting to run her hands through the thick black silk of his hair, to trace a finger over the high cheekbones, the broad nose, the full, impossibly sensual mouth.

She sat so their bodies were just touching and sipped her drink slowly while he played. Toward the song's end, the part where the man builds a house meant for two, T. R. reached for the high notes on the piano, his elbow brushing against her breast so that it burned.

Every sense tingled as her very being came alive with anticipation. It was as if she'd been in a desert and had come upon a well of sweet, clear water. The thought of him, the touch of him, intoxicated and calmed her at the same time. Sitting next to him, she felt all the previous nerves and jitters, the sense of restlessness, take wing and leave her body. It felt so right being here beside him. It felt like . . . home.

It came to her then that she was in love with him. She'd been pushing that realization down, willing it back into her unconscious mind since last week, maybe even since that last night in Hawaii. She'd fought admitting it to her friends and to herself, but there was no more fight left in her. Not since high school—no, not even then—had she experienced this. It was exciting, exhilarating, and more than a little frightening.

He was the wrong man; somehow she was fated to keep choosing the wrong man. But it really didn't matter. She loved him, and all the interior battles that she'd waged, all that self-denial that week in Hawaii, amounted to nothing.

She loved him, and for now, for tonight, it was enough.

After the final pianistic flourish, definitely cornier and more showy than was his usual style, T. R. turned to Kate and nodded. Man, did she look terrific, he mused to himself, soft and sexy and very feminine.

Taking her hand in his, he put it on his knee. "Hello, Kate O'Brien."

"Hi," she said, almost shyly. "Don't you have to keep on playing?"

"Not really."

"Aren't you the—I mean, didn't Carla hire you to play?"

He got it then. Kate was sure he was still a sideman, a free-lancer scratching for whatever living he could get. He should set her straight, he told himself. Even with her assumptions about him, there was no doubt that she was glad to see him, wanted to be with him. He could see it in the warmth in her eyes and the way the tips of her breasts had pebbled at his touch. His fantasy had come true.

Now was definitely the time to tell her.

Hey, Kate, he could say, I'm not really who you thought I was. I'm a millionaire, actually, a pretty solid-citizen type with real-estate holdings and investments and a portfolio of stocks. I kind of fudged over that part.

He could say, I didn't tell you before because I didn't trust you. The thing is, I wanted to get in your pants. I wanted to notch up the high school cheerleader. Also, I was afraid if you knew how wealthy I was, you might come after me for my money, and you wouldn't be the first. So I put on an act.

No doubt she'd listen quietly, and then she'd say she understood, no problem, and lead him off to bed.

In your dreams, music man.

"I can take a break," he said finally. "Come on out to the terrace."

Kate let T. R. lead her out onto the balcony of Carla's lavish condominium. On the way they passed their hostess, who smiled broadly, giving them both the thumbs-up sign. Kate wondered if Carla had hired T. R. on purpose so that she could play matchmaker. It was working. However, come tomorrow morning, she would give her client a lecture on not meddling in other people's love lives.

Kate looked out at the darkness beyond. It was a starless, moonless night, and the heat she felt in her very pores had only partly to do with the weather. T. R. stood behind her, not touching her, but she was so aware of him, she could almost smell her skin burning from the crackling electricity between them.

"I can't believe you're here," she said, leaning on the wrought-iron railing. "Why didn't you tell me?"

"What's the matter? Don't you like surprises?"

He moved in closer till there was barely any air between them. The back of her neck grew warm, then even warmer. "So, this isn't some kind of coincidence."

"You're too clever, *querida*."

Closing her eyes for a moment, she whispered, "Every time you say that, I lose my breath."

He let out a long sigh. "It's all right. I'll catch it for you."

He reached around her and put his hands beside hers on the railing, imprisoning her body. "*Querida, querida, querida,*" he murmured softly, kissing her ear, then rubbing his mouth over the sensitive skin on her neck. "It's been awful not being with you this week."

She leaned back against him and nodded, her heart full; she was so close to tears that her throat had closed up, making speech impossible.

"Let's get out of here," he said.

"Don't you have to stay?"

"You're the reason I'm here. Only you."

She was powerless to fight him, nor did she want to. Ten minutes after she'd entered the party, Kate left on the arm of the man she loved.

In his car he kept looking over at her and smiling as if to assure himself that she was really there.

"Where are we going?" Kate asked.

"That little studio I told you about. It's five minutes from here."

But the five minutes turned into at least twenty as they got caught in the cruising traffic of Wednesday night on the Sunset Strip. Kate looked out her window at the packs of teenagers who strolled by, giggling, posing, necking, smoking, trying to look as tough as possible. All of them favored the color black in their clothing, the girls Dee's age wearing skintight short skirts and thick makeup that—to Kate's way of thinking—disfigured their fresh young faces. Had she ever been that caught up in trying to look older? she wondered, and then answered herself: Of course she had.

"They seem so anxious to grow up, don't they?" she said. "You just want to shake them and tell them to take time to be young, to stay a child. The world will get to them soon enough."

T. R. nodded. "Yeah. My mother used to say, *'Hijo, no te apures.'* 'Son, what's your hurry?' "

"She's the reason you talk the way you do, isn't she?"

"How do I talk?"

"A little like a street kid and a jazz musician, with some *barrio* thrown in. It's a beautiful mix."

"Glad you like it. It's all I got."

Kate wished she could snuggle up next to him and lean on his shoulder, but the seat belt made that sort of intimacy impossible. She had to content herself with folding her hand in his on the console between the seats. "Tell me about her."

"Mama?"

She nodded. "What was her name?"

"Estrella. Star. She was the best. Tiny little thing—not even five feet—and she was very gentle. She had music in her soul. She sang to me every night. Her people were from Mexico originally, and she used to tell stories about growing up in Texas. She was a wonderful cook—she made delicious *chimichangas* and *flautas* and little crisp cookies that I've never tasted since."

"She sounds like quite a woman."

"She was. But my dad, he drank. Most nights he'd come in loaded, and sometimes he would go for me, to beat me up. She wouldn't let him—stood in front of me, her arms spread out, this little thing with all that power. He never laid a hand on her, I'll say that for him."

"And she died when you were ten?"

He nodded. "Cancer. She'd been sick for a long time but kept it from me. What is it?"

Kate felt a few tears rolling down her cheeks and wiped them away with the heel of her hand. "I'm sorry. I'm just thinking about how painful it would be to lose your mother so young."

With a look of puzzled wonder, he said, "No one's ever cried over me before."

More tears filled her eyes, and she reached into her purse for a tissue. It was amazing, but, now that she'd admitted to herself that she loved him, she had no more defenses against the emotions he aroused in her, from sexual awareness to compassion. There was no armor, no protection; it was frightening to feel without a filter.

She took a moment to compose herself, then asked, "What happened after she died?"

"It was just my dad and me. I had an older brother, but he was killed in 'Nam."

"Did your father—Who protected you from him?"

He gave a bark of humorless laughter. "I did, as soon as I learned how. The army kept trying to get the old man into a program for alcoholics, but he was pretty hopeless. His liver gave out when I was twenty. I heard about it when I was playing a gig in Chicago, and I didn't even get back for the funeral." They were stopped at a traffic light, and T. R. looked straight ahead, his brows knit. "I wish I'd made up with him before he died, wish I'd known how to forgive him then. I do now."

"You're all alone, aren't you?" She heard the tremor in her voice as she asked the question, but was powerless to do anything about it.

"Yeah. I'm used to it." He looked over at her and ran a thumb under her lower lid, catching a tear.

"Don't cry for me, Kate," he said, his own voice as hoarse as hers. "It hurts to see you cry for me."

Their destination was an old building near the Whiskey, a nightclub in the heart of the Strip. A top-floor loft had been converted into a spacious studio, and when T. R. turned on the overhead light, Kate saw that a huge skylight made up most of the ceiling. Her eyes took in all the contents of the cluttered room: A rack of keyboards hooked up to a computer, an old upright piano, a set of drums, shelves of tapes and CDs, a small TV, large pads of yellow score paper on a stand, and an old plaid couch with cigarette burns on the arms.

"Welcome to my temporary abode," T. R. said.

"Have you been staying here the whole time?"

"No, just working here. My friend is cutting an album in Japan. What do you think?"

"I have an incredible urge to dust."

He laughed. "Don't you dare. Besides, I promise it's clean."

She felt shy; the feeling of being exposed and unguarded hadn't abated at all. She wanted him to hold her, and then make love to her, but she couldn't bring herself to say that. So she walked around the room, looking at the strange paraphernalia that accompanied music making in the electronic age. "This is a whole other world to me."

T. R. lit a couple of thick candles on the piano, then turned off the overhead light so that the room was suffused with a soft yellow glow. Coming up behind her, he put his arms around her waist. "It's my world, *querida*," he whispered in her ear. "What do you want to know about my world?"

Trembling, she felt herself softening all over. "I don't even know where to begin."

"I think I do."

Running the tip of his tongue over all the surfaces of her ear, he brought his hands up and covered her breasts. As the pad of his thumb rubbed across the spandex material of her top, she felt her nipples pucker and harden instantaneously. She arched her back, sighing, and let her hands fall to her sides, her fingernails scoring lightly over the bunched muscles of his upper thighs.

T. R. groaned as he felt the already aroused flesh between his legs tighten like a drawn bow. Turning her body around to face his, he cradled her head in his hands, gazed into her eyes with all the tender fire that was in his heart, and took possession of her mouth.

It was an intimate kiss that almost shattered her with delight, and Kate heard herself whimpering softly. When he thrust his tongue deeply into her, filling her with an aggressive sensuality, she gave herself over to the moment, putting her arms around him and kissing him back with deep, heartfelt passion, opening to him, granting him all the access he demanded, till they were both panting with need.

Still holding her close, T. R. backed her up to the couch till she felt the cushions at the backs of her knees. "It opens out to a bed," he said hoarsely.

"No," she cried. "Don't stop touching me."

Her knees gave way, and suddenly she was sitting down, feeling dazed and out of breath. She laughed. "I'm lost. I have no idea where I am."

"You're here," he said, pulling off her net top, "with me."

"Oh, yes, that I am," she said, reaching up to unbutton his shirt with quivering fingers.

He helped her, cursing silently as he struggled out of the sleeves, then, bare chested, impatiently pulled the bandeau top over her head. Now Kate looked both shy and wanton, her creamy breasts with their dark, tight peaks rising and falling with each dazed breath. She was impossibly beautiful in the candlelight. He thought he'd go mad with wanting her.

Kate watched T. R. through a sensual haze. His eyes seemed to be devouring her as he fell to his knees and brought his hands to her breasts. He teased the aching tips till they were ruby hard, sending long ribbons of fire down to her loins. Then he leaned in closer, and his teeth raked lightly over her nipple. Her head fell back against the couch, and she threaded her shaking hands into his hair, letting the thick silken strands slide between her fingers as he sucked gently on her breasts.

Soon his hot hands and tongue stroked up and down the length of her, touching, testing, tasting all of her feverish skin. When he pulled at the waistband of her navy pants, she lifted her hips to help him, and soon she was wearing nothing at all.

Opening her eyes, she reached for his zipper, pulling it down past the rounded contours of his arousal and cupping him through his briefs. He pushed her hand away and hurriedly stepped out of the rest of his clothes. He stood over her, looking down at her with primitive passion, the thick, hard evidence of his need for her making it impossible not to reach out and stroke the length of it with her hand.

"Kate," he cried out as he closed his eyes and felt her surrounding him with her velvet touch. It was almost more than he could bear. Sinking again to his knees, he pushed her legs apart and leaned into her, kissing her pouty, trembling mouth.

Kate opened herself to him, inviting him into the gentle heat of her mouth, loving the feel of his tongue rubbing hotly over hers, groaning as she felt his long fingers stroke along the sensitive skin of her inner thighs and then slide upward to find even more sensitive skin. She shivered as his thumb sought and found the aroused nubbin amid the moist womanly folds.

"Oh!" she cried, but the word was lost in a gasp as his thumb moved again, sending lightning through her. Arching up into his hand, she moved her hips against him, urging him on until one long finger slid up and found the hot, soft center of her, moving in and out with insistent strokes until fire melted her.

Just when she thought she couldn't take any more, he released her from their kiss and bent down to replace his hand with his mouth. She was lost; her hips moved with an involuntary rhythm of their own, up and down and side to side as she came apart beneath the sensual assault of his tongue and gently sucking mouth, and she cried out her pleasure as she climbed the peak and soared off into space.

T. R. held tight to Kate as she convulsed against his mouth, loving how freely, how passionately, she responded to him. But he was not through with her, not yet; he felt as if he would burst if he didn't enter her right now.

Reaching along the floor for his pants, he took out the condom from his pocket, and, with shaking hands, put it on. Moving onto the couch and sitting down, he pulled her onto him so that she impaled herself with a passionate cry. He thrust up into her, tightly sheathed in her liquid heat, still feeling the small contractions that followed her climax. At each of his movements, she cried out, digging her nails into his shoulders as she adjusted to his rhythms.

More, he wanted more. He moved again so that he lay back down on the couch, she on top. Her heat rippled around him again, tugging at him. Her busy, restless hands stroked his hair off his face, her nails like liquid flame against his cheeks, his chest, his nipples. As he drove up into her, she leaned over and held him tightly.

She was different tonight. He could sense her body flowing around him, her soft angles around his hard, masculine planes. It was as if she couldn't tolerate any separateness, as if she had to be joined to him. That night in Hawaii she'd been in the grip of a strong attraction that she hadn't wanted to feel. Here, tonight, she was all giving, all consumed with him, her concentration and her enjoyment total, with no regrets, no second thoughts, no inhibitions or barriers. She was all fire, and she consumed him with her flame.

He felt himself beginning to shatter and shifted once more until she was under him, her legs encircling his hips. A scream came from the depths of her slender body as he drove into her again and again and again.

Her eyes opened with surprise as she realized she was going to climax one more time. As she held on to his shoulders, her head twisting from side to side in ecstasy while he shuddered wildly against her, Kate cried out, "I love you! I love you! I love you!"

T. R. was strangely silent on the ride back to Carla's, where Kate had left her car. Although he held on to her hand tightly, he offered short, distracted replies to all her attempts at conversation. It wasn't as if he'd pulled away from her so much as if there was something troubling him that he needed to sort out.

There had been a change in him after she'd cried out her love for him. He'd held her tightly, almost possessively, and after a while he'd made love to her again and then again, the last time bringing her to climax several times before taking his own shuddering release.

But still, even as her body luxuriated in the most lavishly sensual experience it had ever known, she could sense that he was troubled. She kept waiting, hoping, expecting him to say something about his feelings for her. When he didn't, she couldn't help feeling an overwhelming sense of disappointment that he couldn't find the same words she had.

Oh, he felt *something* for her, there was no doubt of that. No man made love to a woman the way T. R. had made love to Kate—cherishing her, worshiping her, putting all the emphasis on her satisfaction—unless his emotions were involved. But apparently his feelings for her didn't run as deeply as hers did for him.

Given her track record, she reminded herself, why should that surprise her?

As they drove along Sunset Boulevard, the sidewalks were quieter but still filled with kids who obviously didn't have a curfew. The passing streetlights cast shadows on the strong planes of T. R.'s face, making the furrowed brows and hollows under his cheekbones darker, more intense than usual.

When he pulled up in front of Carla's hillside condominium and turned off the motor, he turned to her, a contemplative look on his face. "Sure you can't spend the rest of the night with me?"

She shook her head. "Not with work tomorrow. And not with Mom and Dee expecting me. It's hard, you know, when you have people at home waiting for you."

He offered a small, joyless smile. "I wouldn't know."

Once again, Kate experienced that same wave of compassion for the lonely, needy child who lived— had probably always lived—under T. R.'s knowing, assured surface. But she would not cry again, because with the oppressive mood in the car, she didn't know if the tears would be for him or for her. He was going to say good-bye; she sensed it, and some small part of her mind was scurrying away to find relief.

"Kate," he said quietly, cupping her face, "I—Never mind."

"What? Talk to me."

He shook his head slowly. "No. Listen, I have the rhythm section session tomorrow"—his eyes darted to the dashboard clock—"actually, it's today. And the full orchestra on Friday."

"Are you nervous? Is that what's bothering you?"

He shrugged in that no-big-deal manner of his that Kate had come to realize meant a very great deal. "Yeah, maybe a little. The thing is, I haven't asked you to come because you'd probably distract me. Maybe you can make it to the next one."

The next one. She liked the sound of that. It made her smile. "Sure. I'd love to."

He took her hand, lacing his fingers through hers. "Kate, I—" Again, he seemed reluctant to say whatever it was he'd begun to say.

"You what? Don't you just hate it when someone doesn't finish a sentence?" she said lightly.

He studied their still-joined hands. "I was going to say that the evening was . . . very special. That *you're* very special."

There was more, she knew it, but he wasn't about to say it, and Kate wasn't about to force the man into declaring his feelings for her. It would be a little like sending herself a Valentine's Day card. "Yes. It was wonderful, T. R. And now I have to go."

As she reached for the door handle, he put a hand on her shoulder. "Are you sure?"

"It's three o'clock in the morning. I have to get up in four hours."

"It's not safe."

"I'm used to it. When I drive home at night, I keep my door locked and put a real tough expression on my face."

"I'm going to follow you anyway, just to make sure you get there okay."

This fussing over her—clucking, he'd called it when she'd done it to him—she kind of liked it. It felt . . . cherishing. "If you want to, I guess I can't stop you."

He walked her over to her car and then pulled her

to him, wrapping her in his arms while he rested his cheek on the top of her head. *"Querida,"* he murmured. "I'll miss you."

She lifted her head and looked at him. As his supple fingers stroked her hair off her face, he smiled, his eyes like dark sapphires in the shadows of night. "Good luck today and Friday."

"I'll need it," he said, his eyes roaming over her face as if he were memorizing her.

"Do you think you'll make it to Dee's concert?"

His hand stilled, and he frowned. "Damn, I almost forgot. I don't know. I'll try."

She nodded. Laying her head against the smooth silk of his shirt, she wrapped her arms around his waist and hugged him tightly, listening to his heartbeat and wishing the night could go on forever.

Ten

"Mom! Mom! Wake up!"

With great reluctance Kate opened one eyelid and peered at her daughter. Dee was on her knees, bouncing around on Kate's bed, something she hadn't done for many years.

"What time is it?" Kate asked, running her tongue around her teeth and making a face.

"I don't know. About six-thirty, I guess. You have to get up soon, anyway. I've been waiting to talk to you for hours!"

She yawned. "Is there some kind of emergency?"

"No."

"Is Grandma all right?"

"Grandma's fine."

"Then what's so important that you had to come in here like the house was on fire?"

"I know who T. R. is!" Dee said triumphantly.

Kate stifled another yawn. "What are you talking about?"

"T. R. is Ry-No-Mite!"

"Dynamite?"

"No, Mom, Ry-No-Mite." She spelled it out.

Kate wondered if she'd woken up incredibly stupid this morning, or if Dee was into mind games. "Honey, I don't have the foggiest idea what you're talking about."

"Mom!" Dee said again, with exasperation. "That's his name, or his stage name, I guess." She jumped with excitement. "He used to be with Pow!"

Kate had always known there was some sort of language barrier between teenagers and the rest of the world, but she had little patience for it this morning. She fluffed up her pillows and leaned against them, forcing her eyes to open wider. Her lashes felt sticky. No wonder. Between being with T. R. on Wednesday night and missing him like crazy last night, she wasn't in the best of shape. "Dee. Stop moving so much and tell me what you're talking about."

Her daughter looked up at the heavens as though to ask for patience, then unbent her long limbs and seated herself, cross-legged, at the foot of the bed. With exaggerated slowness, as though talking to a small child, she explained. "I'm trying to tell you that T. R. was a member of a really hot band called Pow! P—O—W. Okay?"

"Okay."

"His handle, the name he used, was Ry-No-Mite. All the guys in the band had names like that, you know like explosives, weapons, action kind of names. The lead guitarist was called Rex-Splosion, and the drummer was Billy Bang-Bang. Like that."

Apparently Dee had no trouble pronouncing names like that with a straight face. Amazing. "Okay. So, T. R. was in that band. He was probably in a lot of bands."

"But this was a *famous* one, Mom. Pow! was really big, for like ten years. That's a long time for a heavy-metal group to stay together and to stay on top."

Kate found herself wondering why T. R. had neglected to tell her this piece of news. "If they were so famous, I'm surprised you didn't know who he was immediately." Dee had an encyclopedic memory for everything to do with all rock music since the Beatles.

"I did tell you he looked familiar," she replied, slightly defensive. "But the thing was—his face was never well known. The band all wore these real weird masks when they performed, so you couldn't see what they looked like. Kind of like Kiss, you know?"

A vague memory of leering clown faces and lightning bolts crossed Kate's mind. "I remember Kiss."

"Well, Pow! was almost as big as they were. Of course, you never heard of them, because you won't listen to that kind of music."

"Silly me." Something was gnawing at her, but she couldn't quite bring it to the surface. "So, what happened? How come you found out who T. R. was?"

Dee began jumping on the bed again. "They had a whole show about Pow! on MTV last night, and we were all watching at Ronnie's house, and I screamed when it came on, and made everybody shut up. It was so cool. I told everybody I knew him, and then I was like this big celebrity."

"It was on TV?"

"It was, like, you know, one of those where-are-they-now kind of things." Dee stopped jumping and shook her head. "What a bummer. Rex-Splosion OD'd about five years ago, and that's when the group broke up. The drummer is with another band, and the other guitarist lives in Europe and plays jazz." The last word was said with faint disdain, but then Dee's voice took on the excited edge again. "But the big news is T. R."

"What?"

"Mom, he's, like, a zillionaire! He has this big cattle ranch in Montana, I mean, really big—thousands of acres! And a bunch of other homes, all over the place. He set up this foundation that works with runaway kids. And he went back to school and got a college degree, and then he studied music. Mom, he went to Juilliard! And now he manages a couple of groups and is starting this film score thing, and, well, he's big. I mean, he's really hot!"

Kate was fully awake now, unable to speak.

Dee peered at her with curiosity. "So, why do you think he, you know, didn't tell us? I mean, why would he hide all that stuff about himself?"

Kate looked down at her hands; they were clutching the edge of the blanket. "I don't know."

"Do you think he'll come to my concert tonight? I mean, do you think he'd bother, you know, with kids?" Dee's face always registered everything she was feeling, and right now it was a portrait of young, wide-eyed anxiety.

Kate felt a strong rush of maternal protectiveness toward her and reached over to squeeze her hand. "I don't know," she said gently. "He said he'd try. Is there coffee, honey?"

"Sure. Would you like some in bed, like on Mother's Day?"

"I would very much like some in bed, thank you."

"I could make you some cinnamon toast."

Kate managed a small smile. "Just coffee, thanks."

After Dee skipped off to do her good deed, Kate lay back on the pillows and pulled the blanket up under her neck. As her eyes roamed around her bedroom, the same room she'd inhabited most of her life, she tried to make sense out of all the information Dee had presented.

How did the man her daughter described from the TV show gibe with the man with whom Kate had spent most of the previous night?

Apparently, T. R. was not one of the ninety-five percent of free-lance musicians who barely made a living, although he had certainly led her to believe that he was. Instead, he was extremely wealthy and extremely successful. He'd gone to college and attended one of the most respected music schools in the country, if not the world. Why, then, had he tried so hard to come off as an uneducated, overly casual piano player? Why hadn't he told her the truth about himself? Except for recounting his past drug use, he'd been deliberately vague about everything from high school to the present.

She should have picked up some hint, of course. Maybe she'd been putting so much energy into fighting and then giving in to her attraction to him that she'd not been as mentally swift as usual. Thinking back over their conversations, she realized there had been signs. Always, she had had a sense of him as someone who was not quite what he appeared to be.

T. R. had worn a mask onstage, had he? He'd also worn a mask with her. Why? What possible reason could he have for presenting himself like that?

She felt betrayed. Leaning on one elbow, she reached for the phone. She would confront him right this minute and demand an explanation. But her hand dropped to her side, and she sank back onto the pillows. She had no idea where he was staying. He'd kept that bit of information from her too.

Just two nights ago, she'd been so open, so exposed with him; she'd held nothing back. But this morning, as she lay in bed, her thoughts and emotions churning, Kate could actually feel herself closing up again, covering herself with a protective layer of righteous anger.

T. R. listened to the playback one more time, then looked over at the film's director, who was sitting next to him. "What do you think?"

"Terrific stuff, T. R. Let's move on to the next cue."

T. R. depressed the talk-back button, and said to the conductor in the studio, "Hey, Steve, the strings sound great, and the guitar riff finally works. That's a buy."

The music *was* terrific, and that described the way T. R. felt too. High on himself. He'd worked his butt off to get here, to get this feeling of work well done. The only ingredient missing was Kate. He wished he'd had her there after all, to approve, even to worship him a little. After all, a man liked to show off for his woman.

His woman. Interesting phrase there. But that's how he'd come to think of her, as his woman. T. R. Beltran was finally hooked, thoroughly and completely. As soon as he could get some other business out of the way, he intended to tell Kate O'Brien—his woman—that she had his heart.

He glanced at his watch and frowned. There was no way he would make it to Dee's concert. While he listened to the rehearsal of the next cue with one ear, he picked up the phone and dialed Kate's number. Her machine was on, and he expressed his apology to Dee, told her that he'd make it next time, and left word for Kate to call him at the studio.

Kate saw the light blinking on her answering machine the minute she and Claire got home. After she rewound the tape and heard T. R.'s message, she stared at the machine for a few moments, wrestling with herself. She didn't really want to talk to him. Since Dee's startling news that morning, Kate's feeling of betrayal had grown and she had worked up a pretty good case against T. R. Now, everything he'd ever said to her, every compliment, every fact of his life, was under suspicion.

She wanted him to just go away, out of her life, and let her get on with the business of getting over him. But it was never that easy; she would have to confront him at some point, she told herself, and it might as well be right now.

Seating herself stiffly on the edge of her bed, Kate punched in the numbers.

"Yeah?" said an unfriendly male voice. In the background there was loud music playing.

"May I speak to T. R., please."

"Hold on, we're in the middle of a playback." The phone was put down for a few moments until the blaring music stopped. Then Kate heard the man who had answered yell out, "Hey, T. R. Some chick is on the phone."

After a beat, T. R. came on the line. "Kate?"

"Yes."

"Hold on. Tell the band to take five, will you?" he said to someone in the room, then his tone became more intimate. "Hi. I'm glad you called. How was the concert?"

"Good. The kids always put on quite a show."

"We're running over here, but it's not my fault, thank God. There were technical glitches. But Kate, the director likes my stuff and, at the risk of sounding like I'm tooting my own horn, it sounds pretty good to me too."

"That's nice."

T. R. was puzzled—and hurt—by Kate's lack of enthusiasm. Both yesterday and today had gone well, really well, and he'd wanted to share his sense of accomplishment with her. But there was something in her voice . . .

"Kate? Is everything okay?"

"Why shouldn't it be?"

"I don't know. I kind of thought you'd—Never mind." The silence that followed made him uneasy. "Are you having regrets about the other night? Is that it? Because if you are, don't." He lowered his voice to a whisper. "Being with you, Kate, it was the most special time I've ever had."

"And you've had a lot of special times."

Was it the connection? Her voice sounded so flat, so lifeless. "Not really. I wish I didn't have to go away."

"You're going away?"

"In the morning, to Canada. I just found out about it tonight. I have to—I mean—"

"What, T. R.?" she interrupted. "You have to visit one of your homes? Or maybe dedicate a stadium in your name?"

He winced at her coldness. "Kate—"

"I know who you are, all right? Dee told me—it was all over MTV."

He closed his eyes; a few heartbeats passed before he was able to speak. "So. I've been busted, huh."

"You sure have."

"And you're really pissed off."

"You better believe it."

He nodded. "Yeah, I knew you would be—that's why I kept it from you."

"Great. What a mature thing to do." Her voice dripped with sarcasm. "Knowing someone will be angry at the lies you're telling, you decide to keep lying."

"It's not quite like that. Kate, give me a chance to explain."

"I don't feel like giving out a lot of chances right now, okay? You deceived me. It's like I gave my heart to a . . . fabrication. I did it again, didn't I? Fell for someone about as trustworthy as a crooked politician. I feel so foolish."

"Kate, stop. I want to talk to you, but not like this." He dragged his fingers through his hair. "Look, one of my groups is signing a major contract, and I have to be there. I'll call you from Canada tomorrow night."

"Don't bother."

It pained him to realize how thoroughly she had shut down. "Kate, please," he said. "I love you."

He heard her quick intake of breath; then she

said, in a low, controlled voice, "And that's supposed to make it all right?"

He didn't know how to answer but was saved from having to say anything because she hung up the phone.

On Tuesday morning, having overslept, which made her late for her eight o'clock, Kate dashed up the stairs to Annabella and tripped on the top step. She tried to catch herself on the railing, but she managed to sprawl, unhurt but not pleased, on the landing at the top of the stairs. She lay there for a moment with her eyes closed, thinking that this was not a great way to start out a day.

"Are you okay, Kate?" she heard Bella say. Kate opened her eyes, expecting to see her friend. Instead she saw a pair of men's moccasins at eye level. Letting her gaze travel upward, she took in the slightly frayed hemline of well-worn jeans that tightly encased well-defined calves, thick muscular thighs, and—

"Oh, no." Shaking her head, she brought herself to a sitting position and leaned against the wall. "What are you doing here?"

T. R. squatted next to her, a hint of amusement in his vibrant sapphire eyes. "Opening up negotiations."

"What kind of negotiations?"

"For the purpose of bringing together two warring parties into an amicable agreement."

"Why do you sound like a lawyer all of a sudden? Wait a minute, don't tell me. In between classes at Juilliard, you found time to go to law school."

"Come on." Grabbing her by the shoulders, he pulled her up to a standing position, not letting her go until she shook him off.

"Sorry. I'm not in the mood for negotiations."

"But you'll hear me out."

She raised an eyebrow. "Will I?"

"Yeah. You're getting tired of hanging up on me, and you're not really the type to slam a door without giving me a chance to explain."

She shrugged. "Maybe, but not now. I'm booked up all day."

Bella poked her head out from the kitchen, where she was brewing the morning coffee. "Your eight o'clock canceled, Kate," she said helpfully. "She said she'll pay you for it next week."

For the first time Kate looked around the room to see not only Bella but two other manicurists and their early morning customers, all of them avidly following her and T. R.'s conversation. Turning her back to the room, she looked out a window.

"So," he said, "looks like you have a free hour."

She crossed her arms over her chest. "That doesn't mean I want to spend it with you."

"What do you usually do when you have a free hour?"

"Get a cup of coffee. Go to the bank. Go for a walk."

"Sounds good." He took her arm and hustled her off down the stairs before she had a chance to say no.

The two-story brick building that housed the two Annabellas was located in the Brentwood Country Mart, a jumble of shops around an open courtyard located on the south side of San Vicente Boulevard. The broad avenue was bisected by a grassy median with well-worn footpaths and a line of tall coral trees down the middle. Coming out of the shop, Kate crossed to the median and began to walk west, toward the ocean two miles away, pointedly ignoring T. R.

This early, the August heat was not yet intolerable, and there were several joggers who passed them as, side by side, but isolated, Kate and he made their way in silence for a while. She wore a light cotton sundress and sandals, and her hair was off her face in a French braid. She was pretty angry, and hurt too. He could tell by the way she walked, quickly, her head bent, watching her own feet.

After they'd gone a few blocks, he asked, "Are you ready to listen yet?"

She started when he spoke, then turned her pale blue eyes on him for a quick scrutiny before gazing back down at her toenails. "Okay, talk."

"First off, I'm sorry about my little act. Really sorry."

"Why did you do it?"

"I'm going to tell you that, all of it, the truth. And you're not going to like some of it."

"I'm not too crazy about any of it so far."

"Could we sit down or something?"

She stopped walking and looked over at him again, the distrust on her face so strong, he thought he'd have to perform a miracle to bring her back to the loving, open woman he'd held in his arms only a week ago.

"How about here?" He perched on a thick, gnarled root that spread out from one of the trees, the full green branches overhead affording refuge from the sun. Patting a natural hollow in the brown wood close to him, he held out a hand to help her.

Sitting where he indicated without his help, Kate tucked her skirt around her legs and picked up a blade of grass. "I'm listening."

Best to just get to it, he told himself. "Okay. I didn't tell you who I was at first because—Oh, man, this is going to sound so stupid. The thing is, I wanted you to fall for me—No, I wanted you to hop into bed with me before you knew who I was."

"For heaven's sake, why?"

He leaned back against the tree trunk and closed his eyes. He could hear the cars whizzing by, bits of conversations from passing joggers, the buzz of insects, a dog barking in the distance. "I wanted to be this ordinary guy, this nobody like I was in high school, and have you want me anyway. Back then, I'd look in the mirror and see all these pimples. And I was fat, and no one paid a lot of attention to me, especially beautiful blond cheerleaders. I wanted them to like me, God, how I wanted them to notice me. But they looked right through me, like I was invisible."

"Don't do this, T. R."

His eyes popped open, and he looked over at her. "Do what?"

"Try to get me to feel sorry for you."

"No, no, no. That's not what I'm trying—" He sighed. This was maybe the hardest thing he'd ever had to do. "Look, here's how it was. When I saw you on the beach that day, well it was like I got a chance to do it all over, to change history, and I took it. Especially when you said how much you hated musicians and how you had this principle about not going out with them. It was a challenge, you see?"

"A challenge," she repeated.

"I would be the exception. You would fall for me, get so tied up in knots to have me, that you'd go against your principles. But it had to be for me. Me. Tomás Beltran, the loser, the son of an alcoholic, the kid who couldn't make friends and had no future except maybe to die from drugs and booze at an early age. Does any of this make sense?"

She gestured helplessly. "Sure it does, and I'm as capable of compassion as the next person. Apparently, I was some sort of test for you, to prove your worthiness. And I passed the test, I guess. Or you did. Am I supposed to be happy about that?"

"No, of course not."

She plucked another blade of grass and swiveled it between her fingers. "Okay, put aside for a minute that you wanted to get me into bed. Why didn't you tell me afterward?"

"You're not going to like this part either."

"Why doesn't that surprise me?"

"You kept going on about this dream man, this button-down kind of guy, this steady breadwinner type. I thought that if you knew I was pretty well off, you might let it affect your feelings for me, you know, make you like me more."

"What would be wrong with that?"

"But I wouldn't know why you liked me, you see?"

Understanding dawned on her face. "You mean you thought I might fall in love with you—or pretend to—because you were rich? Like some kind of gold digger?"

"Hey, it's been known to happen."

"Is that how you saw me? See me?"

"No. Well, maybe at first, but only for about five minutes."

"Screw you."

She started to get up, but T. R. held her arm firmly. "Kate, listen. Do you have any idea how cynical you get about love when you're onstage and women of all ages throw themselves at you? How many times a night I could have gotten laid just because of my fame and my money?"

"And I suppose you never took advantage of that."

He let go of his grip on her arm. "In the beginning, sure. I was a kid, and indiscriminate screwing wasn't a matter of life and death then, like it is today. I haven't taken advantage of that kind of easy sex for years. But, believe me, it's still around. And I'll tell you, not one of those women would give me the time of day if I worked for the post office."

She laughed derisively. "Don't sell yourself short, T. R. Women look at you wherever we go. There's a couple of candidates in the salon right now who have no idea who you are or what you do for a living and wouldn't think of asking questions until later. A lot later."

"So, then I'm a sex object, like you women are

always complaining about. See? There's something wrong here. Either I'm wanted for my money and fame, or for what I look like, but never for what I am." The tip of his index finger pushed into his chest as he continued with intensity. "*Who* I am. Inside. Me. Remember that night on the beach when you said you wanted to be taken seriously, and not just be thought of as a blonde with a great body?"

"And that was all the more reason for trusting me sooner," she cried, "for telling me the truth. I poured my heart out to you that night. I would have understood."

"Would you?" he challenged. "With all the prejudices you've worked up over the years? Man, you couldn't stop spouting all that stuff about musicians, how unreliable they were, how this, how that."

"Well, it's usually true, isn't it?"

"Is it? Sure, there's a lot of those guys around, but there's also a lot of guys with kids and a mortgage, regular types who just happen to earn their living playing music."

Kate shook her head. "I've never met any of them."

"You've never been attracted to one like that, you mean. There's a reason for that, Kate, but you'll bite my head off if we talk about it."

Folding her arms across her chest, she said, "Don't you dare stop there. Tell me, why am I attracted to unreliable, irresponsible men?"

"So you can say that all men are that way and have a reason to stay alone," he said quietly. "So you never have to admit that you're scared, and you'll never have to commit and never have to trust."

"Thank you for your insight. You missed your calling, you know. You should have a radio talk show, dispensing advice to the lovelorn. And when you go on a personal appearance and the fans see you, you'll have to beat them off with a stick." Kate got up and, brushing dead leaves off her skirt, headed back toward the shop.

T. R. pushed himself off the ground and caught up to her, touching her shoulder. "Kate, stop."

She shrugged off his hand. "Why?"

"Because we're not finished here."

"I am."

"What's the matter? Truth too painful?"

She turned to him, her hands on her hips. "You're saying that to me? How much truth have I heard from you from the day we met?"

"It's all been the truth. I've never lied, not really."

"Just left some stuff out."

"Yes, and looking at it now, I'm sorry. I was wrong, but dammit, everything I did tell you about myself, my feelings, it was all the gospel truth. Including the fact that I love you."

Despite her attempts at self-control, her eyes filled with tears. "Which you managed not to say when we were together, making love, but put in almost as an afterthought later, when you knew I was going to hang up on you. Tell me honestly, can you blame me for having a little trouble believing you?"

There was such pain in her voice and on her face. What could he say to make it go away? "Kate, I don't blame you for not trusting me. It'll take a little time to convince you."

She shook her head sadly. "The clock just ran out, T. R. You'll never convince me."

Eleven

Kate was only dimly aware of the phone ringing Thursday morning and Bella saying, "Annabella, how may I help you?" and then calling out, "Carla, it's for you."

The lawyer, who was soaking one of her hands in soapy water, picked up the receiver next to Kate's station with the other. "Yes?" she said, then smiled. "Right." She nodded. "Got it. Okay."

Carla gave the phone to Kate. "I'm running downstairs for an espresso, so you can answer this man's question."

"Who . . . ?" she said, taking the phone as the other woman got up from the chair.

But of course she knew the answer even before he said, "So, where did we leave off?"

T. R. sounded as if it had been two seconds instead of two days since they'd last talked, and still his voice brought tears to her eyes. She shook her her head slowly. "I don't know. I'm really mixed-up."

"Yeah," he agreed. "I've been thinking a whole bunch about the two of us. What about if we just start over?"

Kate felt the eyes of the other women in the shop on her, so she lowered her head and kept her voice as soft as possible. "From where?"

"From the beginning. Like we just met on the beach and I say, 'Well, well, as I live and breathe, if it isn't a lovely lady from my past, Kate O'Brien. Hi, Kate. You don't remember me, but I had a big crush on you in high school, and I'd like to wine and dine you.' Something like that."

"And then I would say, 'Tell me, T. R., what do you do for a living?' And you would say, 'I'm a musician,' and I would say, 'I don't go out with musicians,' and we're back at square one."

"Still stereotyping the hell out of each other, both of us."

"What do you mean?"

"Labels. Musicians are unreliable, women in classy bikinis who stay at expensive hotels have to be rich bitches, or gold diggers. Hell, you were even worried I'd think less of you for being a manicurist."

"At first, yes, but then I told you the truth." She winced as she realized how self-righteous she sounded.

"Chalk one up for you. I wasn't so honorable."

"I'm sorry. I didn't mean—"

His chuckle interrupted her. "Sure you did, but it's okay. The thing is, we never gave each other credit for just being who we were, without the labels."

Kate thought about it. He was absolutely right, and she wondered why she hadn't seen it before. "Why do you think that is?"

"For my part, I was scared."

"What of?"

"The same thing you were, I think. Neither of us has a real good track record in the love department. And I guess that's about trust, something we don't do very well."

"I trust," she said emphatically. "I have friends I would trust with my life, and my family too."

"But not men. That's why you're still alone—you're afraid to trust that your heart won't be broken. Hey, same with me. I never let anyone get close enough. Except you," he added softly. "Only you, Kate."

At these tender words Kate felt the tears welling up again, and her breathing became more difficult. He was getting to her, the way he'd been getting to her since that day on the beach. There was something about this man that penetrated her very soul. "Oh, T. R.," she sighed.

"I've done a lot more thinking these past couple of days, and I'm never going to keep stuff from you like that, never again. But you threw me, Kate. I've been alone for so long. I was sure I'd be alone for the rest of my life. Suddenly there you were, and there I was, thinking words like love and babies. Man, it scared the hell out of me. But you know, you were braver than I was. At least you had the courage to admit it, and I—"

"Wait a minute," Kate interrupted. "I'm still back a couple of sentences ago. Babies?"

"Yeah. I want us to make a baby. What do you think?"

"I think you have a very active imagination. And I have to go."

"You're really terrified, aren't you?" he said softly.

"My appointment . . ."

"Carla will stay downstairs till you tell her to come back up."

"No one tells Carla what to do."

"I have a lot of clout with her law firm."

Kate couldn't help smiling. "What am I going to do with you, T. R.?"

"Glad you asked. Uh . . ." For the first time in their conversation he seemed at a loss for words.

He took a moment to clear his throat. "Okay. In spite of my poor timing, I really do love you, Kate. I . . . I would like to marry you."

"Marry?" Kate exclaimed. Several people in the shop looked over at her, and she felt the heat rising in her face. She angled her head away from the others and whispered, "Are you serious? You want to marry me?"

"Call me crazy, but yeah." T. R. smiled to himself. He'd had stage fright before, but this pounding in his heart was worse than the worst nerves he'd ever experienced. "Love equals marriage, at least it used to. And I've never asked a woman to do that before, if that counts for anything."

"Marriage," Kate said again, as though testing the sound of the word. "But we barely know each other."

"Don't we?"

"And I have Dee. And Mom."

"Dee's terrific, and if *you* don't want me, I'll propose to your mother."

"You're serious," she said, wonder in her voice.

"It doesn't get any more serious than this. What do you think?"

"I honestly don't know what to say."

He held his breath. "Yes would be nice."

"Don't, T. R. It's not that easy."

"Why, *querida?*"

"And don't call me that. Can't you see? You're right. I do have a problem with trust, and I really don't know if I can trust you. How do I know you won't lie again—okay, lie by omission—five minutes from now, or five years?"

Her words hurt, but he understood that she needed to say them. "You don't. You have only my word that I'll never lie to you again."

"And how do I know you won't leave, be with me for a while, then need to be somewhere else?"

"You don't know that either."

"I mean, it's not like you have a lot of permanence in your past, right?"

"Right."

"So I'm to take the fact that you love me and want to be with me on faith, and—I don't know—trust that it will all work out."

She sounded panicked; he wished he could find the words to reassure her. "Something like that."

"I have to think about this. I don't think I have that kind of faith, T. R., not when it comes to men."

"Oh, Kate." A deep, wearying sadness came over him. "I'm not 'men.' I'm not a category. I'm me."

I'm me.

T. R.'s words haunted her for the rest of the day. Kate's Thursday clients were an unusually chatty group; today, she was grateful for that. She nodded and smiled at them, filed and painted and polished their nails, and stayed in her head all day.

I'm me.

The phrase came back to her time and time again, like a litany. Other words did too.

Labels. Fear.

Trust.

That was the hardest one of all. To trust not only that a man would be honest, but that, in this day and age, a marriage would work out.

Marriage? She hadn't even thought of that in connection with T. R. Love, yes. Sensuality and sexual fulfillment, definitely. But marriage?

Despair. That's what caring for a man had come to mean to her—despair. How sad that was, she thought. How had she grown into thinking this way?

T. R. had said that in high school she gave off a glow, that she seemed to get a kick out of life. Where had that glow gone? It had been diminished when she'd been abandoned by the first boy she loved. Betrayed by the man she married. Then there was the death of her father. Her mother's illness. All the hard work of raising a child alone.

The death of her dreams.

I'm me, he'd said. Marry me, he'd said.

Kate had thought, in years past, that she would find a safe, conservative man—with no expectations of loving him—and settle down. But she hadn't done that, had she? T. R. had hit it on the nose: She'd had quite a few chances, and hadn't taken one of them.

She needed to face up to herself, to the truth of what was inside. She feared love because in the past it had meant sadness and betrayal.

What did love mean now, today, with T. R.? Did it have a fighting chance?

Kate flinched as the screen door slammed even more loudly than usual. That's it, she told herself. She'd find a handyman tomorrow. Enough!

"Hello, everybody," she called out as she rifled through the mail.

There was no answer, which was strange. The aroma of something delicious cooking on the stove usually greeted Kate when she got home.

"Dee? Mom?"

Still no one answered, so, after tossing her purse on the table, she went into the kitchen. There was no activity there, so Kate looked through the small window in the back door. Mom and Dee were sitting at the wrought-iron ice-cream table in the tiny backyard. T. R. was lying down on the one good chaise, a tall glass of what looked like fresh iced tea on the table next to him.

It was a repeat of last week's tableau—the king and his handmaidens.

She'd half thought he'd give up on her after this morning's phone call. She wouldn't have blamed him if he had. Her lack of faith was pretty thick; a person didn't get over the habit of not trusting overnight, and she didn't know just how much patience he had for waiting around. After all, with his face and body, his fame and wealth, he could have any woman he wanted.

But he wanted her.

He had made that perfectly clear. Whatever it was that they shared, each of them had let the other break through barriers that no one else had ever come close to penetrating. Maybe that was what was so special about the two of them. Maybe their love might just have a chance to survive after all.

Kate retrieved the pitcher of iced tea from the refrigerator and opened the back door. "Anyone care for a refill?"

T. R. turned in her direction and grinned, lifting up his glass. She walked over and filled it.

"Kate, dear," Claire said, "T. R.'s been telling us about his ranch in Montana."

"Mom!" Dee exclaimed. "He has real cattle, like in *City Slickers*! And a big house and a barn and horses. He says if you say it's okay, we can all go and visit there!"

Kate met T. R.'s gaze. "Did he now?"

Claire looked from her daughter to T. R. and then said, "Dee, why don't you come in and help me with dinner?"

"But I thought we were bringing in tacos to-night."

"Then why don't you help me make the call? Now."

"Sure," Dee said good-naturedly as she got up and followed her grandmother. At the door she turned. "Mom, T. R. says he'll be glad to talk to me about the music business and maybe even introduce me to some people, if you say it's all right."

"What else did I say?" T. R. prompted.

"Oh, yeah. I should think about going to college. He says a lot of the guys he knows minored in music and majored in, you know, academic stuff. I might consider that. We'll see."

"Dee," Claire called from the kitchen.

"Coming, Grandma. You're staying, aren't you?" she said to T. R.

He looked questioningly at Kate, who said, "He's staying. Take the pitcher, would you, honey?"

After Dee was gone, T. R. scooted over so that Kate could sit next to him on the chaise. "Hi," he said happily.

"How long have you been here?" she asked as she sat.

"About an hour."

"All that—college plans and tales of Montana and my mother's obvious approval—in one hour. Miracle worker, aren't you?"

"I keep telling you."

Subdued, Kate traced a fingernail over the flower pattern on the cushion and avoided T. R.'s eyes. "I'm . . . glad you're here."

"That's a relief. I told myself that I was an idiot for coming to your house, that I should have more dignity than to run after a woman who keeps pushing me away." He smiled wryly. "But I passed dignity a long time ago. I'm getting off on rejection now."

"Don't, T. R. I"—she took a deep breath and expelled it—"I've been thinking about what you said all day."

"Sounds hopeful. How about we get some dinner, and I talk you into marrying me?"

Her face registered surprise. "Even after everything I said this morning?"

"Even after everything you said this morning." He reached up and stroked some wisps of hair off her face. "*Querida*," he said quietly. "I love you so."

"Don't say that."

"But it feels so good."

"I'm still not sure what I should do."

"Take a chance, baby."

"I did that before."

"But that's when you were a kid, and the guys you picked were kids too. You're a grown-up now, and so am I."

"I hadn't thought about that, but it's true."

"And I got to tell you, I think I'm a catch. I'm talented, I'm charming, and, in all modesty, not a bad-looking guy."

Kate smiled. "Not bad-looking at all," she agreed.

"I'm thirty-five, I'm mature, I'm someone you can depend on. I haven't had an easy life, and I've got a lot of scars, but I'm past all the bad part, I think. It's like I've been wandering for years, since I was a kid, and now I want to settle down. With you. There's enough money, it's steady, and I'll always be there if you need me. Isn't that the kind of man you've been looking for?"

"God, you sound so sane, so sensible."

"Mr. Button-down, that's me."

Laughing, she said, "Please, no."

It was going to be all right, T. R. thought. He knew it for sure now and, his chest expanding, exploding with love for her, he brought her hand to his mouth and kissed the palm. "But I'm still a musician, Kate. It's my life. I'm going to concentrate more and more on the composing, but I don't know what the years will bring. Whatever happens, it will always be about music."

"I know."

"And sometimes I get a little involved and have to change plans. But not too often."

"I know."

"Still got it in for all musicians?"

"Not all of them, I guess. How do you feel about heavy metal?"

"Like it's part of my past. My ears can't take too much anymore."

"Good."

"But you'll let me educate you a little, won't you?" he asked. "I mean, we don't have to listen to Lite Oldies all the time, do we?"

One slender eyebrow arched. "What's the matter? You have a problem with 'Satisfaction' played by the Living Strings?"

"Definitely one of the top ten on my list." He grinned and placed her hand on his chest. "See how easy it is? See how good we are together?"

Kate felt the strong, steady beat of his heart against her palm. "What about the groupies that are always around musicians. Do they tempt you?"

"Kate O'Brien, are you asking if I'll be faithful to you?"

Suddenly unable to meet his eyes, she looked down and nodded.

"I like that you're jealous. Groupies," he repeated thoughtfully. "They seem to get younger every year. And I seem to get older. Besides"—putting his hands under her arms, he pulled her to him so that she was lying on top of him—"if I have you in bed with me at night, I'll never need anyone else."

"You know just the right thing to say."

Kate lay her head down under his chin, loving the feel of T. R.'s arms as they enfolded her, the sure touch of his musician's fingers rubbing away the tightness between her shoulder blades. She was finding it surprisingly easy to relax against him this evening. Each doubt, each question, each insecurity, was being swept away by his confident answers and laid-back manner.

"Do you really want a baby?" she asked.

He kissed the top of her head. "I'd be lying if I said no. How do you feel about it?"

"I always thought Dee would be the only child I'd ever have. But when you said that this morning, about making a baby, I don't know, something inside me got so happy."

He let out a breath. "Yeah, I know the feeling."

"It's just that—" She stopped, uncertain about what she wanted to say.

With his hands on her cheeks, he lifted her head so that she was facing him. "Tell me, *querida*."

"I'm sorry for all the questions. I guess I'm scared."

"Scared to trust me?"

"Scared to trust life, I think."

"Yeah, it's pretty scary."

She rolled off him and lay in the crook of his arm, his heartbeat against her cheek. After a while, Kate asked, "Where would we live?"

"Where do you want to live?"

"Dee has school, her friends. . . ."

"Then we'll live here in L.A. till she finishes. That'll work out just fine, because this is where most of the films are made. Your mother can live with us."

"She's been talking about moving in with her sister. I have a feeling that's what she'll do."

He shrugged. "Whatever."

"What will happen to your place in Montana?"

His fingers combed through her hair, their touch gentle and soothing. "It will stay just where it is," he said with a smile. "There are planes, weekends, vacations. . . ."

"Just like that?"

"Just like that."

"You really do have a lot of money," Kate said.

"Yes."

"I'm not used to that."

He chuckled. "You get used to it real quick."

"I don't think I could ever depend on just your money," she said thoughtfully. "You know what I mean. It would make me too dependent."

"Then you could keep working."

"At the shop?"

"There, somewhere else. But you'd have the freedom to choose."

"I've never had that kind of freedom before."

His arm tightened as he pulled her even closer and kissed her forehead. "There's a lot of things neither of us has had before, Kate. We'll give them to each other, I hope. Those dreams you told me about? You wanted to travel and go to school and read? You'll be able to do that now. You'll be able to go to Italy—with me."

She looked up to find him gazing at her, his eyes aglow with a warm blue fire. "You remember everything I said, don't you?" she asked softly.

"Everything. Including the fact that just a few days ago you told me you loved me. But I haven't heard it since."

She stroked his face with her fingertips. "Oh, T. R., of course I love you. You make it impossible not to."

He kissed her, a soft, sweet kiss that signaled his deep feelings. "And you'll marry me?" he whispered against her mouth.

A quiet peace came over Kate then. She had all the answers she needed, here in the arms of the man she loved. That tight, terrified knot of fear that she'd been carrying around inside for years was gone; it had evaporated into the hot summer night. "I'll marry you," she said quietly.

He kissed her again, his tongue searching for hers and receiving a most loving welcome.

"Mom," Kate heard Dee say as she threw open the back door. It was quickly followed by "Oh. Sorry. Uh, later," the sound of a slamming door, then the exuberant voice of her daughter screaming, "Grandma, Mom and T. R. are necking! It's so cool!"

THE EDITOR'S CORNER

Come join the celebration next month when LOVE-SWEPT reaches its tenth anniversary! When the line was started, we made a very important change in the way romance was being published. At the time, most romance authors published under a pseudonym, but we were so proud of our authors that we wanted to give them the credit and personal recognition they deserved. Since then LOVESWEPT authors have always written under their own names and their pictures appear on the inside covers of the books.

Right from the beginning LOVESWEPT was at the cutting edge, and as our readership changes, we change with them. In the process, we have nurtured writing stars, not only for romance, but for the publishing industry as a whole. We're proud of LOVESWEPT and the authors whose words we have brought to countless readers over the last ten years.

The lineup next month is indeed something to be proud about, with romances from five authors who have been steady—and stellar—contributors to LOVESWEPT since the very beginning and one up-and-coming name. Further, each of these six books carries a special anniversary message from the author to you. So don't let the good times pass you by. Pick up all six books, then sit back and enjoy!

The first of these treasures is **WILDFIRE**, LOVE-SWEPT #618 by Billie Green. Nobody can set aflame a woman's passion like Tanner West. He's spent his life breaking the rules—and more than a few hearts—and makes being bad seem awfully good. Though small-town Texas lawyer Rae Anderson wants a man who'd care for her and give her children, she finds herself rising to Tanner's challenge to walk on the wild side. This breathtaking romance is just what you've come to expect from super-talented Billie!

Kay Hooper continues her *Men of Mysteries Past* series with **THE TROUBLE WITH JARED**, LOVESWEPT #619. Years before, Jared Chavalier had been obsessed by Danica Gray, but her career as a gemologist had driven them apart. Now she arrives in San Francisco to work on the Mysteries Past exhibit of jewelry and discovers Jared there. And with a dangerous thief afoot, Jared must risk all to protect the only woman he's ever loved. Kay pulls out all the stops with this utterly stunning love story.

WHAT EMILY WANTS, LOVESWEPT #620 by Fayrene Preston, shocks even Emily Stanton herself, but she accepts Jay Barrett's bargain—ten days of her company for the money she so desperately needs. The arrangement is supposed to be platonic, but Emily soon finds she'll do just about anything . . . except let herself fall in love with the man whose probing questions drive her into hiding the truth. Fayrene delivers an intensely emotional and riveting read with this different kind of romance.

'TIL WE MEET AGAIN, LOVESWEPT #621 by Helen Mittermeyer, brings Cole Whitford and Fidelia Peters together at a high school reunion years after she'd disappeared from his life. She's never told him the heartbreaking reason she'd left town, and once the silken web of memories ensnares them both, they have to decide whether to let the past divide them once more . . . or to admit to a love that time has made only more precious. Shimmering with heartfelt emotion, **'TIL WE MEET AGAIN** is Helen at her finest.

Romantic adventure has never been as spellbinding as **STAR-SPANGLED BRIDE**, LOVESWEPT #622 by Iris Johansen. When news station mogul Gabe Falkner is taken by terrorists, he doesn't expect anyone to come to his rescue, least of all a golden-haired angel. But photojournalist Ronnie Dalton would dare anything to set free the man who'd saved her from death years ago, the one man she's always adored, the only man she dares not love. Iris works her bestselling magic with this highly sensual romance.

Last is **THE DOCTOR TAKES A WIFE**, LOVESWEPT #623 by Kimberli Wagner. The doctor is Connor MacLeod, a giant of a Scot who pours all his emotions into his work, but whose heart doesn't come alive until he meets jockey Alix Benton. For the first time since the night her life was nearly ruined, Alix doesn't fear a man's touch. Then suspicious accidents begin to happen, and Connor must face the greatest danger to become Alix's hero. Kimberli brings her special touch of humor and sizzling desire to this terrific romance.

On sale this month from Bantam are four spectacular women's fiction novels. From *New York Times* bestselling author Amanda Quick comes **DANGEROUS**, a breathtaking tale of an impetuous miss— and a passion that leads to peril. Boldness draws Prudence Merryweather into one dangerous episode after another, while the notorious Earl of Angelstone finds himself torn between a raging hunger to possess her and a driving need to keep her safe.

Patricia Potter's new novel, **RENEGADE**, proves that she is a master storyteller of historical romance. Set during the tumultuous days right after the Civil War, **RENEGADE** is the passionate tale of Rhys Redding, the Welsh adventurer who first appeared in **LIGHT-NING** and Susannah Fallon, who must trust Rhys with her life while on a journey through the lawless South.

Pamela Simpson follows the success of **FORTUNE'S CHILD** with the contemporary novel **MIRROR, MIR-ROR**. When an unexpected inheritance entangles Alexandra Wyatt with a powerful family, Allie finds herself falling in love. And as she succumbs to Rafe Sloan's seductive power, she comes to suspect that he knows something of the murder she'd witnessed as a child.

In a dazzling debut, Geralyn Dawson delivers **THE TEXAN'S BRIDE**, the second book in Bantam's series of ONCE UPON A TIME romances. Katie Starr knows the rugged Texan is trouble the moment he steps into her father's inn, yet even as Branch is teasing his way into the lonely young widow's heart, Katie fears her secret would surely drive him away from her.

Also on sale this month in the Doubleday hardcover edition is **MOONLIGHT, MADNESS, AND MAGIC**, an anthology of original novellas by Suzanne Forster, Charlotte Hughes, and Olivia Rupprecht, in which a journal and a golden locket hold the secret to breaking an ancient family curse.

Happy reading!

With warmest wishes,

Nita Taublib

Nita Taublib
Associate Publisher

OFFICIAL RULES TO WINNERS CLASSIC SWEEPSTAKES

No Purchase necessary. To enter the sweepstakes follow instructions found elsewhere in this offer. You can also enter the sweepstakes by hand printing your name, address, city, state and zip code on a 3" x 5" piece of paper and mailing it to: Winners Classic Sweepstakes, P.O. Box 785, Gibbstown, NJ 08027. Mail each entry separately. Sweepstakes begins 12/1/91. Entries must be received by 6/1/93. Some presentations of this sweepstakes may feature a deadline for the Early Bird prize. If the offer you receive does, then to be eligible for the Early Bird prize your entry must be received according to the Early Bird date specified. Not responsible for lost, late, damaged, misdirected, illegible or postage due mail. Mechanically reproduced entries are not eligible. All entries become property of the sponsor and will not be returned.

Prize Selection/Validations: Winners will be selected in random drawings on or about 7/30/93, by VENTURA ASSOCIATES, INC., an independent judging organization whose decisions are final. Odds of winning are determined by total number of entries received. Circulation of this sweepstakes is estimated not to exceed 200 million. Entrants need not be present to win. All prizes are guaranteed to be awarded and delivered to winners. Winners will be notified by mail and may be required to complete an affidavit of eligibility and release of liability which must be returned within 14 days of date of notification or alternate winners will be selected. Any guest of a trip winner will also be required to execute a release of liability. Any prize notification letter or any prize returned to a participating sponsor, Bantam Doubleday Dell Publishing Group, Inc., its participating divisions or subsidiaries, or VENTURA ASSOCIATES, INC. as undeliverable will be awarded to an alternate winner. Prizes are not transferable. No multiple prize winners except as may be necessary due to unavailability, in which case a prize of equal or greater value will be awarded. Prizes will be awarded approximately 90 days after the drawing. All taxes, automobile license and registration fees, if applicable, are the sole responsibility of the winners. Entry constitutes permission (except where prohibited) to use winners' names and likenesses for publicity purposes without further or other compensation.

Participation: This sweepstakes is open to residents of the United States and Canada, except for the province of Quebec. This sweepstakes is sponsored by Bantam Doubleday Dell Publishing Group, Inc. (BDD), 666 Fifth Avenue, New York, NY 10103. Versions of this sweepstakes with different graphics will be offered in conjunction with various solicitations or promotions by different subsidiaries and divisions of BDD. Employees and their families of BDD, its division, subsidiaries, advertising agencies, and VENTURA ASSOCIATES, INC., are not eligible.

Canadian residents, in order to win, must first correctly answer a time limited arithmetical skill testing question. Void in Quebec and wherever prohibited or restricted by law. Subject to all federal, state, local and provincial laws and regulations.

Prizes: The following values for prizes are determined by the manufacturers' suggested retail prices or by what these items are currently known to be selling for at the time this offer was published. Approximate retail values include handling and delivery of prizes. Estimated maximum retail value of prizes: 1 Grand Prize ($27,500 if merchandise or $25,000 Cash); 1 First Prize ($3,000); 5 Second Prizes ($400 each); 35 Third Prizes ($100 each); 1,000 Fourth Prizes ($9.00 each) ; 1 Early Bird Prize ($5,000); Total approximate maximum retail value is $50,000. Winners will have the option of selecting any prize offered at level won. Automobile winner must have a valid driver's license at the time the car is awarded. Trips are subject to space and departure availability. Certain black-out dates may apply. Travel must be completed within one year from the time the prize is awarded. Minors must be accompanied by an adult. Prizes won by minors will be awarded in the name of parent or legal guardian.

For a list of Major Prize Winners (available after 7/30/93): send a self-addressed, stamped envelope entirely separate from your entry to: Winners Classic Sweepstakes Winners, P.O. Box 825, Gibbstown, NJ 08027. Requests must be received by 6/1/93. DO NOT SEND ANY OTHER CORRESPONDENCE TO THIS P.O. BOX.

Don't miss these fabulous Bantam women's fiction titles on sale in May

SACRED LIES

☐ 29063-0 $5.99/6.99 in Canada

by Dianne Edouard & Sandra Ware

Authors of MORTAL SINS

A beautiful agent is drawn into a web of betrayal and desire—where she must choose between who to believe...and who to love.

THE WIZARD OF SEATTLE

☐ 28999-3 $5.50/6.50 in Canada

by Kay Hooper

Co-author of THE DELANEY CHRISTMAS CAROL

A magical romantic fantasy!
From Seattle to Ancient Atlantis, Richard Patrick Merlin and Serena Smyth struggle for control of her spectacular gift of magic—defying a taboo so ancient that the reasons for its existence have been forgotten—risking all for an eternal love.

SILVER FLAME

☐ 29959-X $5.50/6.50 in Canada

by Susan Johnson

Bestselling author of SINFUL and FORBIDDEN

The Braddock-Black dynasty continues!
The fires of romance are white hot when Empress Jordan flees to the Montana wilderness...and finds a man as wild as the land around him.

Ask for these books at your local bookstore or use this page to order.

☐ Please send me the books I have checked above. I am enclosing $ _____ (add $2.50 to cover postage and handling). Send check or money order, no cash or C. O. D.'s please.

Name _____

Address _____

City/ State/ Zip _____

Send order to: Bantam Books, Dept. FN102, 2451 S. Wolf Rd., Des Plaines, IL 60018

Allow four to six weeks for delivery.

Prices and availability subject to change without notice.   FN102 5/93